Arrow Book of
SPORTS
STORIES

Edited by TONY SIMON

Illustrated by Tom Eaglin

SCHOLASTIC BOOK SERVICES
NEW YORK • TORONTO • LONDON • AUCKLAND • SYDNEY

ACKNOWLEDGMENTS

"Canoe Race" by Joseph Olgin from *Youth's Comrade* (now *Teens Today*), copyright 1951 by Nazarene Publishing House. Reprinted by permission of the author.

"The Diving Fool" by Franklin M. Reck from THE AMERICAN BOY ANTHOLOGY, published by Thomas Y. Crowell Company. Reprinted by permission of Mrs. Franklin M. Reck.

"Hit the Hoop" by Charles Coombs from YOUNG READERS BASKETBALL STORIES, copyright 1951 by Lantern Press, Inc. Reprinted by permission of Lantern Press, Inc.

"Kid Brother" by B. J. Chute, copyright 1946 by B. J. Chute. Reprinted by permission of the author and *Boys' Life*, published by the Boy Scouts of America.

"The Magic Bat" by Clem Philbrook from YOUNG READERS SPORTS STORIES, copyright 1949 by The Judson Press. Reprinted by permission of Lantern Press, Inc.

"The Mighty Mites" by Charles Coombs from YOUNG READERS FOOTBALL STORIES, copyright 1950 by Lantern Press, Inc. Reprinted by permission of Lantern Press, Inc.

"Mothers' Football Club" by Joseph Olgin from *Teens*, copyright 1953 by The Judson Press. Reprinted by permission of the author.

"Pop Can Wear the Medal," by Mary Coleman Jackson, © 1969 by Scholastic Magazines, Inc.

"Soapbox Race" by Charles Coombs from YOUNG READERS OUTDOOR SPORTS STORIES, copyright 1951 by A. L. Furman. Reprinted by permission of Lantern Press, Inc.

"Surprise Attack" by Joseph Olgin from *Teens*, copyright 1952 by The Judson Press. Reprinted by permission of the author.

"Water Bug" by Charles Coombs from TEEN-AGE CHAMPION SPORTS STORIES, copyright 1950 by Charles Coombs. Reprinted by permission of Lantern Press, Inc.

4th printing .... January 1971

Printed in the U.S.A.

CONTENTS

Hit the Hoop

by Charles Coombs

Wᴇ ᴡᴇʀᴇ ɢᴏɪɴɢ ᴜᴘꜱᴛᴀɪʀꜱ to the court when Jimmy Carter strolled into the locker room.

"Just take your time, Jimmy," I said. "After all, we play Kilgore tomorrow. And they're only good."

Jimmy smiled as he pulled his basketball togs from his locker. "Save me a spot on the bench," he yawned.

Well, Jimmy knew he was safe. For two years he had been the mainstay of the Harding Junior High team. Hardly a game was played in which Jimmy didn't score at least half the points. You don't save a place on the bench for a guy like that — not if you hope to win any games.

Although Jimmy was far from what you would call a "team" player, most of us were willing to overlook his ball-hogging as long as he could lead us to a pennant.

But we hadn't reckoned with the arrival of a new coach. Coach Drake was fresh out of college. He didn't look much older than most high school players. But he sure knew basketball. And I had noticed during our game last Friday how Coach Drake watched Jimmy. Although the star forward had scored twenty-two points all by himself, the new coach didn't seem at all pleased at what he saw.

Now as Jimmy walked out onto the floor a few minutes after the rest of us had begun practice, Coach Drake said, "You're late, Carter."

Jimmy glanced at an imaginary wristwatch. "Guess I am, at that, coach," he admitted lightly, as though it was beneath him to give it a second thought.

Jimmy wasn't trying to be cute, I'm sure. He was sometimes afflicted with a warped sense of humor. Coach Drake's face turned sort of beet-red.

"Take two laps around the track, Carter," he said sharply. "And make them fast laps."

Kim Clark, Steve Miller, and I exchanged troubled glances. Jimmy was a little on the bullheaded side. We wondered what would happen. Would he do as the new coach instructed, or would he turn in his suit? Jimmy knew he was good. Sometimes maybe he crowded the idea a little too much. But he usually backed it up by hitting the hoop at regular intervals. I held my breath. If Jimmy quit the team, we could kiss all of our hoped-for victories good-bye.

"I said, make them *fast,* Carter," Coach Drake prompted.

Jimmy's face was white as library paste. Without a word, he headed for the stairs down into the locker room. My heart was pounding in my chest. Then, at the last moment, Jimmy turned right and disappeared out the side door toward the running track.

The team was saved — temporarily, at least. But I knew that Jimmy was too stubborn a guy to take much of Coach Drake's disciplining. He had been getting away with things too long. And, after all, there was no rule saying that Jimmy had to play basketball for Harding Junior High.

Jimmy didn't look so very tired when he returned from his two "fast" laps around the track. I imagine Coach Drake noticed it too.

"Carter," the coach beckoned to him, "fill in at forward on the second string for a while."

Jimmy was just peeved enough to play hard. He shot and dribbled as though the ball were on a string. Even those of us who had played two seasons with him couldn't form a good defense against his downcourt attacks. But Coach Drake didn't appear overly impressed.

"Now, let's have a team that will work together," he told us. But it was quite plain that his words were directed primarily at Jimmy.

The following afternoon we played Kilgore. Coach

Drake started Jimmy in his regular forward position. Jimmy rushed in at the opening whistle. He took Steve's center tip, feinted the ball to Kim, then started his dribble. In the meantime Steve raced straight down the court, outdistanced the Kilgore guard, and drew up under the basket in the open.

"Pass, Jimmy!" he called.

Jimmy hesitated a moment. There was no doubt that he saw Steve — saw also that Steve was open for a shot. But Jimmy didn't pass. He dribbled all the way down the floor, pivoted around a guard and flipped the ball up and through the hoop. I glanced toward the bench and saw the dark displeasure on the coach's face.

A couple of minutes later Jimmy made another lone romp down the full length of the court. He sank the basket, all right. Then Larry Roberts came romping onto the floor.

"Roberts for Carter!" the referee announced.

Well, Jimmy played the rest of the game from the bench. We lost by three heartbreaking points. There was a glum silence in the locker room. We figured that the new coach was being too hard on us — Jimmy in particular. We could have won the game, I was sure, had Coach Drake left our sharpshooting forward in the game.

Maybe the look on Jimmy's face wasn't exactly what you'd call smug. But he *did* look as though he was thinking along much the same line I was.

We barely skinned out with victories in our next two games. Jimmy was allowed to play a part of each one. While he was on the floor, he scored quite regularly.

But he didn't seem to have any intention of laying off his one-man dribbling and shooting forays. Nor did Coach Drake seem to have any intention of letting him keep it up. Consequently, Jimmy played the better part of each game from the bench.

I began to wonder if Jimmy would get in enough time to earn his letter. At Harding Junior High, a three-year letterman was presented with a special sweater at the end of the year — you know, a regular letterman's sweater with three stripes around the sleeve, just like they do in high schools and colleges. That was about as big an honor as you could get at Harding Junior High. Few rate it. Jimmy had been one of those few — until recently.

On the following Friday we took the court against Hillview. We were nervous. The Hillview game is always an important one. This year it was even more so, since we had dropped quite far down in the Conference standing.

As usual, Coach Drake gave Jimmy first chance by starting him. "I want to see lots of passing out there," the coach said. "Watch for the man in the open!" As usual, it was a rather direct warning to Jimmy.

The first time Jimmy got the ball, he started going places. Now, I'm not sure that he intended to dribble the entire length of the court. Not so soon after the coach's warning. Jimmy's no dummy. But there didn't seem to be a man in the clear right at the moment, so he dribbled. Two Hillview men were on him like a flash. But Jimmy was like a flea on a hot stove. He pivoted and swung away from the Hillview players, dodging and weaving. About that time Kim cut in from the left side, streaking for the basket, and leaving his guard flat-footed.

But if Jimmy saw Kim, he didn't let on. He kept right on dribbling, leaped high into the air and flicked the ball through the hoop for two points.

It was all very neat. The crowd cheered. However, Coach Drake wasn't one of the cheering crowd. I saw him turn to Larry Roberts. Larry soon loped onto the court. Jimmy turned and shuffled disgruntedly toward the bench. He looked puzzled. After all, he had scored that basket in the very opening seconds of the game. Still, Jimmy couldn't have been so unaware of why he had been benched. Coach Drake didn't say a word to him. The game continued.

But what a game! With Jimmy out of the way, the Hillview team had little trouble in controlling the ball, and less trouble finding the basket. By the end of the first quarter, they led us 14 to 6.

I felt sure that Coach Drake would send Jimmy back in. Even if Jimmy was a one-man player, I figured the coach was practical-minded enough to overlook it just for this one game — this one *big* game.

But it may be that Coach Drake figured there was something even more important at stake, for when the second quarter began, Jimmy was still on the bench.

We were really getting tired out there on the court. We were playing our hearts out, but it was a losing bat-tle. I felt sorry for Larry. Hard as he tried, he couldn't plug the gap that Jimmy's absence had created. Larry lacked something, but it surely wasn't effort. He rated "A" in that.

We switched from man-to-man to zone defense. We put two guards on their sharpshooting center. We tried long shots and short shots. Nothing worked, and Hillview led 26 to 14 at the half. We were an exhausted and sad bunch of boys.

In the locker room I could see that something was bothering Jimmy plenty. Probably he realized that he was losing his letter, as well as his three-year sweater. The rest of us were more concerned with winning the pennant for the school. However, I think we had slowly come around to Coach Drake's way of thinking. Someplace along the line, I suppose we all knew that Jimmy would have to be stopped in his attempts to be a one-man team. But when Coach Drake had taken over the chore, we had been so used to seeing Jimmy get away with it that we had naturally shared some of his resentment.

It was almost time to go back out for the second half. Coach Drake hadn't mentioned any new changes in the lineup. Jimmy might have been expecting to be sent back in.

Finally, he could hold back no longer. I thought there was an unusual amount of moisture in his eyes when he lifted his head out of his hands and looked at the coach.

"Coach Drake," he pleaded, "you've got to put me back in. I won't hog the ball. I promise!"

"Seems that I've heard that story before," the coach said. "Sorry, Jimmy, but we just can't take the chance. The fellows are beginning to work better together out there now. The second half may be an entirely different story. Now, Jim," the coach turned toward the forward, "you've got to guard closer when that man — "

"You won't be taking any chance, coach," Jimmy cut in. "If you'll just let me try again."

"Sorry, Jimmy," the coach said. "Just wouldn't be fair to the others."

I think Jimmy was finding out how much he loved the game. Now he didn't seem to be thinking so much about himself. I figured that he really wanted to get in and straighten out the trouble he already had made.

"Listen, coach," he pleaded. "Please. If you'll put me back in and I don't play the way you want — for the team every second, I — well, you won't need to give me my letter or sweater."

That was a plenty strong promise for Jimmy to make, considering how he wanted and how hard he had worked for his third year letter and sweater. Still, Coach Drake didn't show any signs of relenting.

"Tell him, Dan," Jimmy turned to me. "Tell him to believe me."

"I'd like to, Jimmy, but — "

"I'll turn in all my letters — football and baseball, too — if you think I'm a hog for credit." Jimmy was really near to tears now.

Coach Drake looked from one to the other of us. "All right, Carter," he said. "If the team will vote you in one-hundred per cent, you can go back in to start the second half. Now then, fellows, how many of you think Jimmy deserves another chance out there?"

Jimmy held his breath. Our hands went up, one by one. Even Larry Roberts was a good enough sport to know that Jimmy was our chance, if he played with us. Larry's hand went up.

The coach forgot his pep talks. Jimmy snagged the tip-off. He took just two dribbles, then whipped a pass over to Kim. Kim to Steven to me. Me to Jimmy to Brick. Just like that! Two points!

"Hey, that was really something!" Jimmy grinned.

Then we were at it again, passing that ball as though it had handles on it. And Jimmy could hit a dime with his passes. We hadn't had much chance to find that out before. He was really playing!

By the end of the third quarter the score was all tied up. Hillview was being run ragged trying to figure out who needed the most guarding. Before, all they had to do was tie up Jimmy. But now everybody else was doing the shooting. And each of us was hitting the hoop.

The final quarter was a ding-dong battle. The score see-sawed. But during the last thirty seconds I skidded a sharp pass to Jimmy just outside the free-throw circle. Ordinarily he would have whirled and lobbed a one-handed hook shot at the basket. Not now — now he whirled, all right, but he didn't shoot. He zipped a nice pass squarely into Kim's outstretched hands. Kim flew through the air and dropped the ball smoothly into the webbing.

That was it! Harding Junior High 42; Hillview Junior High 40. Everyone went wild — everyone from Harding, that is.

Not until we were back in the locker room did it dawn on me that Jimmy hadn't shot a single basket during that entire second half. If he realized it, it certainly wasn't bothering him. From the broad grin on his face, he seemed to have discovered something else which gave more pleasure than shooting baskets.

Jimmy turned to the team. "I — I sure want to thank you guys for your — er — vote of confidence in me," he stammered.

"You came through," I grinned. "You earned it."

"I hope so," Jimmy said seriously. "But it was really fun anyway. The best ever."

Yep, all you had to do was to look at him, and you knew that Jimmy's mind was far from worrying about his own personal score, or about sweaters or letters.

At long last Jimmy seemed to have learned the real fun of five fellows playing together in a solid working unit — known far and wide as a *team*.

Water Bug

by Charles Coombs

RANDY MASON could see that his father was trying to hide the worry in his eyes. The drought had put a troubled look into the eyes of a lot of Midvalley farmers.

Randy tried not to think of it, as he buttered a slice of toast. This was the time to be thinking of the coming Cedar Lake Water Carnival. It meant two weeks of free camping in the mountains for the club that won the most points in the swimming carnival. The Bears were counting on those two weeks — counting on Randy.

Randy's father had promised to let him practice this week at the Y.M.C.A. pool in town. And his father certainly wasn't one to go back on his word, drought or no drought.

Yes, Randy was trying desperately not to think of the trouble the drought was causing on the Mason farm.

"Hey, Randy!" It was Tom Carson at the back door. "We'd better get going. Oh, hello, Mrs. Mason — Mr. Mason. We're sure counting on Randy for plenty of points in the swimming and diving events."

"Good morning, Tom," said Randy's mother. "Have you had your breakfast?"

"Yes, thank you, Mrs. Mason. Don't want to eat too much when we're going swimming. How about it, Randy, got your chores done?"

Randy looked over at his father. "How about it, Dad?" he said. "Anything you want me to do today?"

"You go ahead, son," his father said. "I want you boys to get those two weeks in the mountains. Does a fellow good to get away from the farm once in a while."

"We'd never do it if we didn't have Randy to beat Norbert Billings," Tom offered. "Norbert's a member of the Royals, you know."

Mr. Mason nodded, although it was doubtful that he had given the fact much thought.

"But Randy can take him," Tom went on, "if he keeps himself in form this week. You ought to see Randy dive, Mr. Mason."

"I've seen him at the reservoir, Tom," Mr. Mason said. "He's pretty good, isn't he?"

"Oh, that board he rigged up at the reservoir!" Tom said with slight distaste. "You should see him from a *real* board like they have down at the 'Y,' Mr. Mason. He can really swim too."

Mr. Mason smiled. "Quite a water bug, I take it."

"Yes sir. That's it. Randy's a real water bug — come on, Randy, let's get going."

Randy left the table thoughtfully and went outside with Tom. He started for his bike, but he walked slowly.

"What's the matter, fella?" Tom said. "You feeling all right?"

"Tom," Randy turned, "I — I don't think I'd better go today."

"You don't — hey, what goes on?" Tom looked horrified. "You've got to. Norbert'll skin you at the carnival if you don't get in plenty of practice. The guy's good. And those judges are tough. What's got into you?"

"Dad's going to irrigate the alfalfa today. He needs help, Tom."

"But he said it was O.K. for you to go."

"Sure, I know. But — well, that's Dad. This drought is causing a lot of trouble to us farmers, Tom."

"Yeah, I know, Randy. It's tough. But you know the Bears are counting on you. Can't your dad get along — just for the rest of this week?"

"He could," Randy said, "but — well, there are other things that should be done too. He hasn't said so, but I know." Randy's thoughts were organizing themselves. "I've got to stay, Tom. I'm needed here more."

"You're needed at the carnival too, Randy." But Tom was less emphatic. He seemed to see that Randy's mind was made up.

"I'll be there," Randy said.

"A lot of good it will do."

"I'll get in some practice."

"Where?"

"Here."

"Oh, sure. In the irrigation ditches, and that half-drained reservoir, I suppose."

"That's right."

Tom was crestfallen. "Well, I've got to get going," he said resignedly. "I'll break it easy to the fellows." Then his hand was on Randy's arm. "Cheer up. There'll be other carnivals. Maybe I'd do the same thing if my folks had a farm."

Tom, trying to hide his disappointment, got on his bike and rode out of the yard toward town.

Randy's father didn't say much, but Randy couldn't miss the pleased look on his face. "It would be a big help," he said, "if you would handle the irrigating. At nine o'clock we'll be getting water from the Co-operative. Run it in the big ditch toward the north forty. And you'd better boost it a little with about fifty inches from the reservoir."

Randy wore his swim trunks under his overalls. He got a shovel from the tool shed, and headed for the north forty. He just had time to get the check gates set when the water from the Valley Co-operative began to fill the ditch. He went to the weir below the reservoir and added approximately a fifty-inch stream to the supply.

For the next two hours, Randy worked in the hot sun to get the water flowing evenly down the alfalfa panels.

With everything under control, it was a case of watching for breaks in the ditch, and changing the water as each panel filled.

In the waiting time, Randy peeled down to his trunks, jumped into the water-filled ditch, and practiced swimming against the current. The ditch was narrow and he had to keep his arms pretty well tucked in during the crawl stroke. But, anyway, it was practice. He was glad none of the fellows were around — especially Norbert Billings. They would have howled to see him trying to swim in the narrow ditch.

Irrigating was a twenty-four-hour job. Randy's father appeared in the field with lantern and shovel a full hour before he was due.

"How's it going, son?" he asked.

"Fine, Dad," Randy said. "Only got away from me once. But not for long. Hey, you're early, aren't you? Did you get enough sleep?"

"Plenty. Thought maybe you'd like to get in a little diving practice in the reservoir. I've done the milking."

Randy smiled. His dad was a great guy. But, then, Tom was right. The board he had rigged up at the reservoir wasn't very good. Besides, half the water was out of the reservoir.

But Randy went to the reservoir anyway and practiced his dives for nearly an hour. He reached the house just as it was getting dark. Off near the north forty, he could see his father's lantern bobbing as he channeled the precious water.

Randy went to bed right after supper. He would have

to be up at five in the morning to take his shift at the irrigating.

It went that way for the next three days. Tom came to the field one evening, looking very downcast.

"Norbert has been burning up the water at the 'Y' pool," he said. "Doesn't look good, Randy — not good at all. You'll be at Cedar Lake tomorrow, won't you?"

"Sure. We finish up here this evening."

"Well, even a couple of seconds might help," Tom said without conviction. "We need you, Randy. The fellows are feeling pretty low about our chances for getting that outing in the mountains."

"We saved a lot of alfalfa, Dad and I," Randy said proudly.

"Sure, sure," Tom said. "We can't argue against that."

"Besides, I've been keeping in practice," Randy insisted.

"Yeah," Tom said flatly. "I know."

The next morning Randy's father said, "How'd you fellows like me to drive you to Cedar Lake today? Thanks to your help, we're pretty well caught up around here."

"That would be great, Dad!" Randy said. "The fellows will be tickled to save the bus fare."

All the Midvalley boys' clubs were well-represented at Cedar Lake — the Royals, the Bears, the Cougars, the Crimsons. Excitement was high, for every club was after that much-coveted outing in the mountains.

The 400-yard four-man freestyle water relay and the diving were the two final events on the program. With Norbert Billings in top form, it began to look like certain

victory for the Royals. With the two final events left, the
Royals led by three points: 36 to 33.

"Norbert's almost a cinch for the relay as well as the
diving," Randy overheard someone say. He was probably right too. Norbert had spent a good part of the
week in the 'Y' pool and ought to be in top form.

The water in Cedar Lake was exceptionally low, and
the small buoys had to be moved farther out to accommodate the 100-yard distance from shore. The two outward
legs were started from the boat dock, but the two inward legs were water starts — from treading position at
the buoys.

Randy and Norbert were swimming anchor lap. They
treaded water side by side as the race got under way.

Link Larson of the Bears got off to a rather poor start.
He couldn't seem to get his bearing on the buoy. With no
guide ribbons to keep him on a straight course, he got to
weaving around. Every time he looked up to get his bearings, he lost precious seconds. Some of the others were
having the same difficulty. They couldn't seem to swim
in a straight line.

Link arrived at the buoy in fourth place. Del Rankin
lost another three yards on his leg by not being able to
keep on a straight line. Tom came plowing through the
water toward Randy on the next to last lap.

"Oh, boy," Norbert crowed near by, "this is going to
cinch it for the Royals. Too bad, Randy." But Norbert's
voice was lacking in sadness.

"Come on, Tom," Randy yelled as he treaded water
anxiously.

Tom looked up, straightened out his course, and

surged through the water in a powerful crawl stroke.

Tom was blowing hard when he reached out for Randy's hand. Norbert had already taken off, and had a good five-yard head start.

"C-couldn't keep a straight course," Tom apologized quickly.

But Randy was starting his stroke. He looked up just once. The spray from Norbert's butterflying feet caught him in the face. He gained. Norbert seemed to be having the same trouble as the others keeping on a straight line.

Randy forgot everything but swimming. He poured on all the power he had left in his arms and legs. Dully, he could hear the growing crescendo of noise from the beach. He was sorely tempted, but he didn't look up to see if he was still on course. It would take up costly seconds. He had to trust to his judgment.

Randy's arms and legs felt like heavy, aching, water-logged stumps when he finally felt the scrape of sand on his chest. He jerked up his head just in time to see Norbert Billings splash to the beach — in second place.

The Bears were all over Randy, pummeling him happily. Norbert stood aside gasping for breath and scratching his head.

"How did that boy ever keep on his course like that?" someone said. "He looked up only once — at the first of the lap."

It was an hour before the diving event — the final event of the day. The Royals, even with Randy taking first in the relay, still led by one point. The winner of the diving would cinch it.

Randy was rested by the time the loudspeaker called the contestants to the diving platform.

"Because of the drought," the announcer warned, "you undoubtedly have noticed that the water is low in the lake. There's a bare seven-foot depth below the diving platforms. All contestants are cautioned to take that fact into consideration."

"It's a muddy bottom," Randy said. "Seven feet should be enough." But he wondered. A foot or so made a lot of difference when it came to diving. A fellow needed plenty of depth.

Norbert looked worried. "The 'Y' pool is nine feet deep off the board," he complained. "How can they expect us to — "

But soon they were taking their turns from the board. The judges busied themselves over their scoring cards, as one contestant after another went through the designated forward and backward dives.

Then they moved to the high board. There was an unusual amount of splashing by the contestants. The judges seemed puzzled at the high percentage of poor dives.

But Randy was having quite a field day. Each of his dives brought a generous round of applause.

"Look at that fellow go!" Tom cried jubilantly.

Randy's final optional dive was a cut-away. He hardly left a splash.

"Right into the shallow water!" Tom said unbelievingly.

There was a short pause, followed by the voice of the announcer on the loudspeaker.

"In the final event of the day — diving — first

place is unanimously awarded to Randy Mason of the Midvalley Bears. And, folks, it looks as though that gives the two-weeks' outing to the Bears. Congratulations, fellows, and — "

No one heard any more. Randy was mobbed, joyously.

Norbert was among the crowd. He was a good loser. "How in the world did you ever manage to keep your head out of the mud, Randy?" he said. "The rest of us had to cut our follow-in short. Mostly too short. Too much splashing. You hardly moved the water."

"The — the only thing I can figure," Randy smiled, "is practicing in our reservoir."

"Practicing in your reservoir? But what's that got to do with this?"

"The drought," said Randy. "Our reservoir is only half full. Pretty shallow. Had to be careful."

And just then something else explained itself to him. He had been puzzled by the way he had been able to swim the straight course in the relay. Now he knew — but he wouldn't dare tell anyone. Who would believe it? Swimming in the narrow, straight irrigation ditch had given him just the practice he needed!

Randy looked up and saw his dad standing proudly on the outskirts of the crowd. The distance wasn't so great, though, that he missed his dad's wink.

Randy felt mighty good. It seemed that a lot of things had been accomplished during the past week.

The Mighty Mites

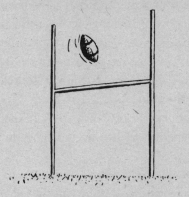

by Charles Coombs

IT SEEMED TO BERT EVANS that the toughest time of the year to be a little guy was during football season. That was when the big fellows rule. If you weren't big enough to be a tackle or a guard, no one seemed to notice you. If you weren't tall and fast enough to make an end, you just weren't in the swim. Or, if you didn't have the muscle and weight to back up your line plunges — well, Bert just didn't qualify for any of those. He was just a shade over five feet tall. He weighed a few ounces shy of ninety pounds. He had muscles, all right. But, for that matter, so did a humming bird.

Yes, the fall season was a tough time for Bert. It was

especially tough because, despite his size, Bert liked to play football.

His single ray of hope was that he wasn't the only one in Walton City who had the same problem. Right now, as he trotted across the grass of the public playground, he found cheer in the size of five other boys — all about his own size — who were tossing a football around at the far end of the field.

"Hey, you're late, Bert." Little Ike Simmons flipped him the ball, made wet by the morning dew still on the grass.

"Had a few chores to do," the small quarterback explained. "Don't worry, I'll be all warmed up by the time those fellows from Lincoln Heights get here."

"They're not coming," center Chubby Reid said. "Some church picnic today that they're all going to."

"Golly," Bert groaned, "then we won't have any competition."

"Naw," Chubby said, "and I was figuring on beating them today."

They had been so busy talking that they hadn't noticed the six big boys who had come wandering up the path. Now there were loud laughs. They whirled around to see six football players from their own school, Walton Junior High, standing nearby. All six of them — big fellows — had amused smiles on their faces.

"You twerps must be talking about checkers," big Moose Spencer laughed. "That's about the only thing you could beat anybody in."

"Oh, yeah?" stocky little Tony Hilton came right back. "Size isn't everything, you know."

"Lucky for you guys it isn't," said Jocko Potter, star end for the junior high Giants.

"Come on," Speed Gains, Giant quarterback, prompted, "let's not waste our time talking with these little half-pints."

Bert could feel the hair along the back of his neck sort of crawl. If there was anything that made him mad, it was to have some big guy making fun of his small size. It was just six times as bad when they made fun of his five teammates too.

He could see that Chubby and Ike and Tony — Don Foss and Freddie Drake too — felt the same way. They all seemed to be trying to hold their tongues. After all, common sense would tell them not to tangle with the six big stars of the junior high team — six fellows who called themselves the Giants.

But Bert wasn't quite so successful at holding back the words that arose in his throat. "You guys are just on your high-horse because you lost your last two games," he challenged.

"Oh, yeah?" Moose Spencer jutted his big chin out.

"Yeah!" Chubby Reid stepped up beside Bert. He got way up on his tiptoes in order to look as big as he possibly could. "Maybe you guys are big as houses. But whoever heard of houses winning a football game?"

"Take it easy," Freddie Drake whispered. "Those guys will break us in half."

"Let 'em start breaking." Ike Simmons puffed up. "I still think they play football like a bunch of rina — rhinocer — hippopotamuses."

The big fellows didn't look so amused now. They had

hardly expected such an outburst from six boys whose total weight was probably little more than half of their own. They didn't seem to know exactly what to make of it. The little fellows were right. They — the Giants — had lost their last two games. Important games too. And both times they had had a large weight advantage. It had worried them plenty. But they had tried not to show it. It seemed that these six small fellows knew it.

It was then that Bert got his big idea. "Look," he said, "if you guys are so hot, how about trying to beat us?"

"Hey, take it easy, Bert," Freddie Drake cautioned quickly.

The six members of the Giants just laughed.

"Bert's got a good idea there," said Chubby. "Only you've got to play our rules. Right, Bert?"

"Sure."

"Your rules?" Speed Gains laughed. "I can just imagine what your rules would be. No tackling, no running, no blocking, no — "

"Our rules are the same as anybody's rules for six-man football," Bert insisted. "They're all pretty standard."

"Six-man football?" Moose Spencer said thoughtfully. "I've heard of it, but never played it."

"Wouldn't hurt to try," his teammate, Jocko Potter offered.

"Yeah," Chubby taunted. "And if you could possibly beat us, at least you could say that you've won one game in the past month."

"You'd better button up that lip," Moose warned.

"Don't make them mad, Chubby," Freddie Drake cautioned. "They'll be plenty tough as it is," he added.

Speed Gains turned to his five big companions. "Shall we show these tiny mites a few things about football?" he asked.

"Might as well," Jocko agreed. "It won't take long."

"Okay, you guys, what are your rules?" Speed asked.

"Well, we've got the field pretty well marked out already," Bert began. "Those sticks lying along the sideline are about fifteen yards apart."

"Fifteen yards? Why?"

"In six-man football you have to make fifteen yards in four downs to keep the ball. Not ten. I guess that's because it's easier to make yardage in touch football than in tackle."

"Hey," Moose objected, "you mean we're not going to get to tackle you guys?"

"That's what he means," Chubby put in. "In six-man football, you just have to tag the ball carrier. You'll have to save your tackles until you play Westside next Friday. Then you can tackle someone your own size."

The six Giants glanced at each other. Even the mention of Westside Junior High was a tender point. The Westside Panthers were big fellows too. Next week's clash was figured to be a really rough one. And if the Giants didn't beat the Panthers, to all intents and purposes they would be through for the season.

"Go on," Speed prompted, "tell us more about your rules. I don't suppose you can even pass the ball."

"Sure, you can pass," Chubby put in. "You *have* to pass."

"What do you mean, 'have to pass'?"

"Boy, you guys are dumb."

"Here's the deal," Bert went on. "In six-man football, at least three players of the team with the ball have to be on the line of scrimmage when each play starts. Usually they are the center and the two ends. The quarterback, halfback, and fullback make up the backfield. Now, when the ball is snapped from center, whoever gets it in the backfield can't run with it across the line of scrimmage."

"Man alive, how crazy can games get!" Moose jeered.

Bert ignored Moose's interruption. "The backfield player who receives the ball from the center cannot run across the line of scrimmage. He first has to pass it — not *hand* it, remember — but pass it to one of his teammates. It can be a lateral or a forward pass. Long or short, it doesn't matter. Just so it's passed, not handed."

"That's right," Chubby came back again. "And everybody on the team is eligible to catch passes. Even the center, like me."

"Boy, oh, boy, what a game!" Jocko Potter laughed. "How sissy can touch football get?"

"You sure won't think it's sissy after you've played it," little Ike Simmons defended. "Wait until we throw a few blocks into you."

Moose laughed. "Oh, you do allow blocking, do you?"

"You're darned right. You'll see."

"Well, let's get going," Speed Gains rubbed his hands together and tried to look ferocious. "We've only got time to score about a thousand points on you. I've got a lawn to mow at home."

"Speaking of points," Bert said, "they're a little different from regular football."

"Awah!" Moose wailed. "What next?"

"The touchdown counts six points, just as in any football game," Bert went on. "But the conversion after touchdown counts one point only if made by a pass or a run. If you drop-kick it or place-kick it well, that counts two points."

"Anything you say, pal," Moose shrugged in resignation. "Come on, let's get to playing."

"The one other difference in scoring," Bert went on, "is that a field goal counts four points instead of three."

"Our goalposts are a little closer together than they should be," Chubby put in. "But we couldn't find a crossbar that was twenty-five feet long — that's how far apart the posts are supposed to be — so we did the best we could. We did get the crossbar spiked up there nine feet from the ground, though, which is correct."

Ike tossed a coin.

"Heads!" Speed called.

"Tails it is," Ike announced, pointing to the coin on the ground. "Okay, Bert, what'll it be?"

"We'll receive," Bert said. Because he was quarterback, he was considered the unofficial captain of the team.

The Giants were given their first surprise right off the bat. Speed kicked off. The ball sailed end over end down the field. Freddie Drake caught it and started straight up the field. All six of the Giants bore down on him. But Freddie was fast. He and the other five smaller fellows had practiced a lot together. Just before Moose reached him, he stopped in his tracks and slipped a short lateral pass to Bert. Without taking two steps, Bert spun around and threw a long lateral to the far side of the field. None of the Giants had even noticed Don Foss waiting over there near the sideline.

Don caught Bert's pass and romped easily all the way to the goal.

"Hey!" Speed Gains shouted, when he realized what had happened. "Why didn't that halfback — "

"You don't have a halfback on that side," Bert reminded, smiling. "But if your fullback, Hollis, had been awake, he would have spotted Don. You've got to pick your man in this game, or you're sunk."

The Giants didn't seem to find tagging the ball carrier as easy as they had figured. Once Moose forgot himself and tackled Freddie hard. Freddie got back to his feet, trying to hold onto his smile. But just to show that he wasn't afraid, he threw a hard block on Speed Gains a couple of plays later. Speed crashed to the ground, looking very surprised that such a little fellow as Freddie Drake could block him to the ground.

As the game went on, the Giants got farther and farther behind in the score. It seemed that with five fewer players on the team to depend on, they were almost powerless to stop the smaller team's tricky attacks.

By the end of what they decided would be the first quarter, the Giants were trailing by four touchdowns: 34 to 7.

"Boy, oh boy." Moose lay down on the grass and mopped the sweat from his forehead. "This is sort of different from what I expected."

"It's a lot different from regular eleven-man football," Bert smiled. "You've got to be on your toes all of the time."

"You can say that again," Speed smiled tiredly. "And you have to do almost twice as much running."

"You learn to dodge, instead of just barging through for an extra yard, like you do in regular games," Chubby said.

"Yeah, that's right," Jocko Potter agreed. "And it sure isn't easy."

Bert chewed on a blade of grass. He looked from one to the other of the six bigger boys. They didn't seem nearly as belligerent as they had about an hour ago. Bert was almost sorry that he and his friends were beating the Giants so badly. It just didn't seem quite right. None of his small teammates was gloating over it either.

After all, the Giants were playing a much different game than they were used to. New rules and everything. They were the ones whose job it was to uphold the glory of Walton Junior High.

It just wasn't much fun to see them all tired out and puzzled about being beaten by six boys so much smaller than themselves.

"Well, let's get started on the second quarter." Speed rolled over and got to his feet. "We'll try to give you guys more competition."

Those were strange words from the usually cocksure Speed Gains.

"This six-man football is quite a game at that," Moose

admitted. "I haven't done so much running in a long time."

"I've been watching how you guys run your plays," Jocko Potter said. "I think I've got the idea better now. So you want to be careful from here on out."

Jocko wasn't far from right. Realizing that steamroller tactics were of no use in six-man touch football, the Giants began to pass the ball around gingerly and to run with a lighter tread in order to shift easily and intercept the dodging tactics of the six smaller boys.

By the end of the half, the Giants had moved up to within two touchdowns of the smaller team: 40 to 27.

During the fifteen-minute rest period, all twelve of them sat under the shade of a big elm tree, talking and laughing together and having quite a time.

Bert and his teammates were elated. The Giants weren't treating them as though they were just a bunch of little pip-squeaks anymore.

But the game took a sudden change in the second half. The Giants, good athletes to begin with, had solved most of the tricks of the six-man game. They began to pass and run the ball with a new speed and agility that left the six smaller boys almost flat-footed.

"Hey," Chubby Reid panted heavily as the smaller team lined up on defense, "those guys aren't half as clumsy as I figured they'd be."

"They're getting better, all right," Ike admitted. "Well, knuckle down and hold them."

But that was easier said than done. The Giants seemed to have found their stride. During the third quarter they passed and dodged and just plain outplayed the smaller boys. They seemed to have discovered a new source of speed in their large bony bodies.

Bert and his teammates were no longer any match for the six junior high players. The big fellows began to romp around them. They weren't using steamroller tactics either. By the end of the third quarter it was the smaller boys who were all tired out. And the Giants led by a score of 48 to 40.

"Hey," Moose Spencer grinned, "this can be a lot of fun at that."

Bert looked at Chubby and smiled. But Chubby looked worried. It wasn't likely that the smaller team would get back in the lead during the final quarter. And if they didn't, they would probably have to take a pretty stiff razzing from the Giants. Chubby didn't seem to be looking forward to that. The game had become a lot of fun — more fun than they had expected, playing six big fellows like the Giants — and the small center didn't relish any more razzing.

"Let's give our all!" Chubby whispered, as the two teams went back to start the fourth quarter.

And they did their very best. But Speed and his teammates were on to the game now. They didn't have much trouble running the score up to 64 to 50 before the game was over.

"Wow!" Jocko Potter yelped. "What a score! Looks more like a lesson in arithmetic."

"Touch football scores usually run pretty high," Bert explained. "Short field, six players on a team, and stuff like that. Makes a fast game."

"Well," Chubby seemed to be bracing himself. "You guys really beat us."

But the razzing didn't come. Speed Gains grinned. "It was a lot of fun," he said. "Maybe we'll try it again sometime."

Pretty soon everyone started home.

Friday afternoon the Walton Giants and the Westside Panthers were having a nip-and-tuck battle on the football field. Each team put everything it had into smashing at the other's line. Bert and his five teammates sat in the bleachers watching the strange tug-o'-war between the two powerful teams. Neither team seemed able to get any place.

"Why don't they try some passes or something?" Bert said soberly. "Golly, they played better against us than they are against the Panthers."

At the end of the first half the Panthers led 20 to 14. As the Giants came back out after the half-time rest period, Speed Gains spotted Bert and his five pint-sized friends. He walked over to them.

"Just watch us this half," he said softly to Bert. "We're really going to give those Panthers a surprise."

The second half started. But it was a very different Giant team out there playing now. They suddenly became fleet-footed. They passed and dodged and stopped depending on their weight to carry them through.

The heavy Panther team was caught flat-footed. They had never known the Giants to play anything but a crushing, charging game. Now they didn't know what to make of this new method of playing.

And while the Panthers were still puzzled, the Giants scored three quick touchdowns, to get into a 34 to 20 lead. The second half was fast and exciting, but the Panthers just weren't able to cope with the Giants' new tactics.

In the bleachers six happy boys cheered wildly for their school team. They cheered loudly for the bigger boys who, only a few days earlier, had made fun of their size.

Caught completely off guard by the Giants' playing, the Panthers went down to a 41 to 20 defeat.

After the two teams had cheered each other, the six main players of the Giant team raced over to where six smaller boys were coming down out of the bleachers on their way home.

"Hey," Speed Gains shouted, "what's your hurry? We want to thank you guys for helping us beat the Panthers today."

"Us?" Bert said, puzzled. "What do you mean?"

"You showed us how we should really play," Moose grinned. "Golly, we were just using our size to barge through. We weren't using our heads. If you fellows hadn't shown us how to play six-man football the other day — well, we'd just never have beaten these guys. Look what happened in the first half."

"Aw, you just hadn't got started right," Ike said.

"Baloney," Jocko Potter said. "We were getting walloped."

"Then I said, 'Let's try doing what those little guys showed us the other day,'" Speed added, "and look what happened!"

"You really did help us win the game," Moose insisted.

The six players looked at one another happily. The Giants were giving them credit for helping their school win the victory!

"If you'll keep helping us, I'll bet we can win the championship," Jocko said. "How about another game one of these days soon?"

"Sure," the little fellows chorused. "Any time at all."

"Great!" Speed said. "How about Saturday?"

"It's a deal."

"Hooray!" Moose cheered. "Saturday the Giants will again play the — the — say, what do you fellows call yourselves, anyway?"

Again the boys looked at one another. They had never really thought of a name. They had hardly considered themselves a football team. But now the Giants called them a team!

"Maybe we should call ourselves the Mites," Bert said finally. "Because we're small."

"Yeah," Ike grinned. "We're the Mites."

"That's not a bad name, I guess," Speed Gains said. "But if it's okay with you, we'd rather call you the Mighty Mites!"

Mighty Mites! Boy, it really sounded good the way Speed said it.

And the way all the fellows were grinning at one another, it really didn't matter what their names were. From now on they were going to have fun together.

Soapbox Race

by Charles Coombs

THERE WERE "SOAPBOX" RACERS of all sizes, shapes, and colors parked at the top of Proctor Hill. More than a thousand spectators, young and old, crowded closely beside the roped-off 900-foot strip of downhill pavement.

It was Soapbox Derby Day in Riverdale.

In the "pits" at the top of the hill, Chubby Lewis worked slowly and methodically to get his entry ready for the next heat — the semifinal. He had his racer canted up on one side, in order to adjust his double-drag brake.

"What you need is ballbearings, not brakes, if you're thinking of winning this next heat," Flash Corby called over from the adjoining pit.

Chubby smiled uneasily. Bearings of any type were ruled out in soapbox competition, but Flash was using every legal method he could think of to add speed to his entry. He had found out that walnut oil is often used by jewelers for lubricating fine watches. Flash had lost no time in mashing some walnuts in order to get a thimbleful of the rare lubricant for his axles.

And now Flash's hands were splotched with dark greaselike patches. "I just finished rubbing it down with graphite," he explained, sounding very professional. "Dirties it up a little, but that's okay — cuts down on wind friction, you know."

Well, there was no doubt about it. Flash had many ideas when it came to eking out the last split second of speed from his racer. Flash had always been a speed demon. He had been the first boy in town to have a Zipper motor on his bike. He was always the one to take first place in the speed events at the model-airplane meets. He was star sprinter on the Riverdale Junior High track squad. No wonder he had acquired the nickname of Flash.

Now, with the all-important semifinal heat coming up, Chubby wondered numbly if he could possibly beat Flash. Would he have a chance to represent Riverdale in the forthcoming All-American Soapbox Derby? It was conducted annually in Akron, Ohio — and to be in it was the greatest honor of all.

"Will the four contestants please line up for the semi-final heat," the loudspeaker blared.

"Here it is, Chubby," Flash grinned. "Be sure you don't let that wheeler get over into my lane. Don't want you tangling up in my rear wheels.

Chubby was trying to think of a clever comeback when a shadow fell across his racer. "Oh, hello, Coach Tom," he smiled up at the big ex-Penn State grid star. Coach Tom was Riverdale Junior High's athletic mentor. But his interest in student doings went beyond sports. He was also a friend to the boys.

"Hi!" said the coach. "Say, you boys are doing all right. Semifinals, huh? Pretty nice!" He poked his head into the flared out cockpit of Chubby's racer — flared out in order to accommodate Chubby's size.

"I see you're using a tiller for steering," Coach Tom commented with definite interest.

"He has to," Flash chimed in. "Chubby couldn't put both himself and a steering wheel into one of these things."

Chubby didn't think that was very funny.

"And a double-drag brake," Coach Tom went on. "That's a good idea, Chubby. I knew a boy once who — "

Well, Chubby thought, Coach Tom seemed to know a lot about soapbox racers. Maybe he had built them once himself. He was the kind of person who would.

"He doesn't need a double-drag brake, Coach Tom," Flash piped up again. "What he needs is a tow rope — or wings."

"Don't be too sure, Flash," Coach Tom smiled.

Chubby didn't miss the open admiration on Coach Tom's face as he turned to get a look at Flash's entry. Flash, within the limit of the official derby rules, had spared no effort in the building of his fleet-lined racer. Flash had slim hips. He had been able to build a needle-like streamlined body — and still fit into it.

Beside Flash's sleek racer, Chubby's entry looked like a bathtub on wheels. Yet, for some reason he had been able to survive competition all the way to the semifinals.

But this was the first time he had been up against Flash Corby. And the prospects of beating him were dim indeed.

After wishing all four entrants good luck, Coach Tom started down the hill in order to be at the finish line when the race ended.

Soon, at the starter's "Ready!" the four boys hunched low behind their curved plastic windshields.

"Get set!"

Suddenly the starting blocks were jerked simultaneously from beneath the wheels of the four racers. They fairly leaped forward down the steep decline that got the 900-foot race off to a fast start.

Flash's racer streaked forward to take an immediate lead. The other two racers clung closely behind him in their respective lanes. Chubby was in last place.

But starting in last place was something to which Chubby had become accustomed. Gravity usually had to work a little overtime to get a good hold on Chubby's weight. But, once it got its grip —

Chubby hunched low, bringing the rim of his crash helmet in line with the top of the windshield. Now there was a continuous rounded surface to cut down wind resistance.

The roar of the crowd was loud in his ears. Flash was already more than a full length out in front. He turned his head and flashed Chubby a confident grin.

Keeping his eyes straight ahead down the course, Chubby suddenly saw people milling around near the finish line. Some seemed to be running around wildly. Strange actions, but this was no time to be worrying about what was taking place beyond the finish line.

There was still the race to win. Jubilantly, Chubby saw that one of the crosstown entries was dropping slowly back. Gravity was now pulling Chubby downhill at an ever increasing speed.

The wind whipped at his cheeks and smarted his eyes. He blinked back the involuntary tears and wished he had a pair of racing goggles like Flash's.

Chubby estimated his speed at between 25 and 30 miles per hour. Plenty fast when you're in a tiny home-made racer that is hardly six feet long and only a few inches off the ground.

Then the second crosstown entry began to drop out of sight behind Chubby's left rear wheel. New courage swept through him. Only one racer was ahead of him now — Flash Corby's.

Even though the gap between them was slowly decreasing, Chubby realized numbly that he couldn't close it completely in the remaining hundred yards. Flash seemed to know it, too, for he turned his head, just enough to toss a triumphant grin at Chubby.

The finish line was rushing toward them.

"Come on!" Chubby pleaded desperately to nothing in particular.

One of the crosstown racers began creeping back up in the lane to his left. Chubby bobbed forward as best he could, in order to pick up a fresh surge of speed. But the close confines of his cockpit made this rather useless.

The roar of the crowd was now louder than ever. Chubby was even with the rear wheels of Flash's racer and creeping slowly forward. They were almost wheel to wheel when the white stripe of the finish line flashed beneath them.

There was no doubt that Flash had won the race. Chubby knew he had come in a close second. But second place in this race was not better than third or fourth, really. Only the winners would be entered in the final event to be run off about an hour later.

These despairing thoughts so occupied Chubby's mind that he forgot about the strange confusion beyond the finish line that had caught his attention when they were halfway up the hill. Now he looked ahead and saw a new activity, as the people scattered wildly from the path of the oncoming racers.

Suddenly Chubby knew why. As the ranks opened, a truck and trailer loaded with cases of soft drinks loomed straight ahead. The threat flashed immediately in Chubby's mind. The truck was stalled right in the middle of and crossways to the race course. Evidently the driver had figured he could get across in plenty of time to clear the safety zone. But he hadn't allowed for the possibility of the ancient vehicle suddenly becoming stalled.

He was fewer than fifty feet away when Chubby jammed his foot down hard on the short crossbeam controlling the drag brake. The twin chunks of old tire rubber he had used for facing grated with a squealing sound on the macadam. Through it, he could hear the drag of the brakes on the other racers.

Then he saw a square dark piece of material bound away from beneath Flash's car. He knew it must be the rubber traction tip from Flash's own single-drag brake. Evidently Flash had failed to check it before the race. All Flash had now was a single piece of bare wood to stop him. It wasn't enough.

As Chubby's racer came to a grinding stop barely ten feet away, Flash ran smack into one of the truck's rear wheels. His momentum wasn't quite enough to throw him from the cockpit or cause him any injury. But it was enough to demolish the front end of his racer.

Chubby slid out of his own racer and rushed over to Flash. Flash stood beside his entry, surveying the damage and biting hard on his lower lip.

"I — I'm sorry, Flash," Chubby consoled. "What a tough break!"

"On the subject of breaks, did you check that brake well before the race, Flash?" It was Coach Tom beside them again. "The other racers were able to make their stops in time."

"No, I — I didn't, Coach Tom," Flash admitted solemnly. "But I didn't think there was any need for — "

"Speed can get you a lot of places, Flash," Coach Tom said. "In a hurry, too, both in racing and in life. The real problem, Flash, is to know when to put on the brakes and to have brakes that will hold. Come on, let's see if this thing can be put together in time for the finals."

But they found after a thorough survey that it couldn't be done — not in the allotted time.

After a lot of thought on the part of the officials, the public address amplifier blared forth again.

" — and due to the untimely and unfortunate accident, it will be impossible for Flash Corby, the winner, to enter the finals. It is, therefore, part of the ruling that the boy who placed second will race in substitution. Chubby Lewis will race in the outside lane and — "

"Flash," Chubby offered quickly, "you use my racer."

"Not a chance, boy," Flash tried to smile. "What happened was my own fault. I'll win next year. Wait till you see the set of brakes I'll have. And I'll know how and when to use them. Come on, I'll help you get ready, Chubby. You're a cinch to take the final."

They started back up to the top of the hill together.

The Magic Bat

by Clem Philbrook

Two DOWN. First of the ninth, with runners on second and third. Fourth game in the series for the City League Championship. We were one game behind already. I glanced at the scoreboard as I stepped into the batter's box. It read: Slaughterhouse Sluggers 3; Grocerymen 2. Our one run lead wouldn't be enough, not with the Grocerymen battling the way they were.

"We need this one, Marty old boy," the gang chattered behind me. "Give it a ride!" Our supporters in the stands chanted for a hit.

I was tense in my stance. Gallo took his stretch. The pitch — and I watched it whistle by for a called strike. I turned my shoulders into the next one. Too late, for strike two. I began sweating. After a glorious .350 season average, I'd fanned my way to a .100 average so far in the series.

The gang was silent behind me. Gallo checked second and third; took his stretch. It came in, chest high and outside. I leaned into it hard, heard the smack as it hit the catcher's mitt. Three strikes are out in anybody's ball game.

Bugs was waiting for me when I trotted toward left field, via his shortstop position. He was munching on a juicy apple.

"Phooey," he muttered between slurps. "You couldn't hit a basketball with a barn door!"

I eyed him coldly. "You are a fine one to be talking. You've bobbled five bloopers in the last three games for a total of eight unearned runs!"

"Seven," Bugs corrected, aiming an appleseed at my shoe.

"Phooey to you too," I growled, trotting on to my position.

Gallo led off, delivering the goods for the Grocerymen to the tune of a double. Dawson came up and singled. It looked as if Tanglefoot was in trouble. "Eight of us right behind you, Tangle old boy," I chattered. "Give 'em both barrels."

He did, retiring two hitters on six straight pitchers. The boys perked up. I came in close for Smith, the Grocerymen's clutch hitter. The stands were hushed as Tan-glefoot took his windup.

The pitch — and Smith swung hard. I heard the sharp crack, saw the ball rifling toward short. Bugs rabbited to it, stumbled, and the pill squirted from his glove. He pounced on it, whirled, fired to Skitch at home plate. The throw was wild and so was the crowd as Gallo scored, with Dawson close on his heels. And that was the ball game. Series standing, 3-1.

Bugs and I lingered after the gang had gone. All I could do was sit there and think about us as we had been. We had begun the season like a house afire, win-ning a dozen straight. We were the toast of Plainfield in those days, the pride of the many friends and business-men who had donated uniforms and equipment.

"We can't let them down, Bugs," I said savagely.

His nose twitched. "I can't figure out what happened to us," he said mournfully.

"Overconfidence. That's what happened to me. I got so cocky over my season average that I couldn't hit any-thing, except a slump. I began missing, more and more. And now I don't have enough self-confidence to climb out of it."

"What you need," Bugs grunted, "is a little pep talk from Ted Williams. There's a boy who has brains enough to snap out of a slump, instead of wallowing around in it permanently."

"While we're tossing bouquets," I retorted, "you could stand a little fatherly advice from Alvin Dark. I don't think he'd have much trouble curing you of dropsy."

It stopped there. We were too downhearted to wrangle.

The following morning at ten o'clock, it happened. When I came back from downtown I found the package by the mailbox. It was long, like the boxes flowers come in, but heavy and well wrapped. A separate stamped envelope pasted on the box was addressed to me.

I tore off the wrappings and lifted the cover. Inside was a baseball bat. One look at the note and my knees began trembling so that I had to sit down on the porch steps. The note read:

Dear Marty:

As a subscriber to the *Plainfield Daily Bugle*, I protest what I'm seeing on the sports page. What gives?

Maybe the enclosed bat will help you out of your slump. Give it a little co-operation, and you're bound to come through.

Best of luck,
TED WILLIAMS

I must have sat there half an hour, just fondling the bat, hefting it, caressing the many indentations which probably represented home runs off world-famous pitchers.

Finally, I became aware of a sound, like the approach of a wailing siren. I discovered it was merely Bugs, streaking up the street, howling my name at the top of his lungs. He took the hedge at one hop and was beside me, panting like a dog in August.

He waved a piece of paper before my nose. "Tell-al-dar," he gurgled.

I lifted an eyebrow. "You don't say?"

He was practically hopping up and down by now. With visible effort he gained control of his vocal cords and made a fresh start. "A telegram from Alvin Dark!" he chattered. "He takes the *Daily Bugle*. He read about my fielding slump." He held a hand at arm's length and examined the nails breezily. "I might add that he has quite a few nice things to say about me."

"Poof!" I said, snapping my fingers. I produced my bat and the note. "And what do you think of this!" I countered triumphantly.

After reading it, Bugs flashed his toothy, impudent grin. "I think," he chortled, "that the Grocerymen have their work cut out for them this afternoon!"

Which was no idle boast. The Grocerymen couldn't get a ball past the infield that day. Bugs was all over the place. Balls just stuck to his glove like lint to my blue serge suit. And his scoopers to second were clicking for beautiful double plays. It was the old Bugs again, back in stride.

As for me, I lashed out for two doubles and a home run for three times at bat.

We took the Grocerymen 7-0, and the gang soon learned about the telegram Bugs received and my bat. There was victory in the air from then on. I carried the bat with me everywhere I went for fear something would happen to it. When I went to sleep that night it was safe and sound under my bed.

The next day we really lived up to our name, and evened up the series of three all. I got two doubles, a triple, and a homer in four times at bat that day. That piece of timber could do everything but run bases.

The afternoon of the final decisive game, interest in the series was at fever pitch. Everyone in town who could run, walk, or crawl was in the stands.

The Grocerymen showed right off they could bounce back from a couple of trouncings. They nicked Tanglefoot for a three-run first inning, then proceeded to match us run for run, right up to the ninth. When the smoke cleared away after their final turn at bat, they led us by two runs.

"Things could look brighter," Skitch groaned.

"What are you worrying about?" Bugs sniffed. "Just wait until Marty gets up there with his magic bat."

"Yeah," put in Hop Riley, "but will he? These babies are fighting hard, and Marty is fifth in the batting order!"

"Well," Tanglefoot said, hitching up his pants, "here goes one man on for you, Marty. I'll be waiting on base for that homer of yours."

Good old Tanglefoot! He made good his boast, scratching out a single. Enthusiasm rose briefly, then waned, as Hop flied out to deep center. Faces were strained when Bugs went down, robbed of a hit by a fluke shoe-string catch.

There was bedlam in the bleachers but we were silent as Skitch strode to the plate. One out now would erase all our effort.

Skitch waited, bat poised. Gallo checked Tanglefoot on first, took his stretch. It was his bullet ball, down the groove. Skitch swung, and the sound of a splintering bat filled the air. Skitch legged it for first and Tangle for second. It would have been a long hit, except for the broken bat. Instead, the ball dropped just behind the third baseman. Safe all around.

The boys were all yelling as I reached for my bat. Even I was certain now of victory. I had a bat that couldn't miss.

But the bat wasn't where I'd left it. In the excitement I must have let someone toss it in with the others by mistake. I rushed over and pawed frantically through the pile. It wasn't there.

Then I accidentally kicked the bat Skitch had just broken, and I went kind of numb all over. Skitch had used — and broken beyond repair — my magic bat!

"On the ball, Marty," Bugs chattered, coming over to me. "You're — " He eyed me more closely. "Hey, what's wrong? You sick or something?"

I held up my bat. "Broken," I groaned. "We're licked."

The boys were gathering around to see what was delaying things. "Take another one," Bugs chirped. "They're all alike."

"*Alike!*" I returned sharply. "That bat put us back in the running. It hit every decent pitch that came near it. Ted Williams used it, and you have the nerve — "

"Fruit cake," Bugs interrupted.

"Huh?"

"That's what you're nutty as," Bugs sniffed. "That bat

came from Mac's Sport Shop, right here in town. All it had ever hit, up to the time you got it, was a few toss-up flies to scar it a little."

I stared, dumbfounded, as the truth dawned. "You mean, you — ?"

"Who else?" Bugs supplied with an irritating grin. "If you had bothered to check, you'd have found out that the package was postmarked right here in Plainfield."

I exploded and snatched up Bugs bodily, as the gang began chuckling.

"Put me down!" he shrieked, threshing air wildly. "It worked, didn't it? You snapped out of your slump, didn't you?"

I paused, then released him slowly. It was true! I was hitting again, and it was not because of a charmed bat. It was due solely to my own ability.

"By the way," Bugs called airily, as I strode for the plate, "you owe me three dollars for that bat."

Gallo didn't stand much chance. Fortified with newfound confidence in myself, and spurred by Bugs' smug grin, I laced the first pitch out of the park for a three-run homer, the game, and our first City League title.

Only one thing marred our victory celebration. Bugs was having too good a time chortling over his cleverness in putting one over on me, and periodically reading his Alvin Dark telegram to any unfortunate who happened by.

I seized a lull in conversation to cut Bugs down to size.

"Belfry!" I jeered at him.

"Huh?"

"That's what you have bats in," I said disdainfully. "That telegram is as phony as the Ted Williams' note."

Bugs stiffened and his eyes bulged. "You?" he croaked.

"Who else?" I grinned. "If you had checked, you'd have seen that it came from Plainfield."

His ego deflated almost visibly.

"By the way, Bugs, old pal," I said, "you owe me seventy-five cents for that telegram."

Surprise Attack

by Joseph Olgin

DANNY MOORE, captain and peppery second baseman of the Webster High baseball team, had just finished breakfast when Tommy Drake, the shortstop, came tearing in, wildly excited.

"D-Danny, g-guess what happened?"

"Take it easy, boy," counseled Danny. "It's spring vacation. We've a week to relax."

"B-but, Danny, I tell you."

Danny smiled indulgently. "What's happened? Did Herb Score register at good old Webster High, knowing that we need a pitcher?"

Tom's face broke into a wide grin. "Something like that. I just saw him. But his name's George Herbert. What a fast ball! It sizzles and smokes!"

Danny grabbed Tom by the arm. "Listen, stop kidding me!"

"I'm not," protested Tom. "He just moved here yesterday. Danny, wait till you see him. It's too good to be true."

Danny prayed inwardly. Visions of the league championship began dancing in his head. He'd just about resigned himself to a mediocre season — the team's veteran hurlers had graduated, and there wasn't one promising pitcher in the new crop. Then Danny forced himself to face stern reality.

"Let's go, Tom," he said, grabbing his glove. "I want to see this new wonder before I go overboard in my dreams."

When they arrived at the ball park, Tommy steered Danny over to a tall, husky boy who was lobbing the ball to Gabby Francis, Webster's talkative catcher. Gabby's face was beaming.

"We're in, Danny!" he shouted. "We've come up with a real fireballer!"

Danny stared at the newcomer as he was introduced. George towered almost a foot over his own five-foot-four stature. Danny felt dwarfed as the big fellow's gigantic paw smothered his hand. George seemed amused.

"Sure pick your captains small," he smiled.

Danny felt a twinge of annoyance — but personal feelings didn't matter now. If the big lug could pitch . . .

"Let's see what you have on the ball," he ordered tersely.

George stretched, reared back, and delivered. Danny gasped as the white pellet exploded into Gabby's glove with a smack that was heard all over the field. Danny forced himself to be calm.

"Got control?"

George shrugged his shoulders. "Ask him," he said, pointing to Gabby.

Gabby's voice rose eloquently. "He can thread a needle at two hundred yards!"

"Let me have the mitt," asked Danny.

"Careful — you're a little guy," cautioned George. "I'm gonna burn 'em in!"

George's next pitch almost tore Danny's hand off. The big fellow had the fastest ball Danny had ever seen. A sharp-breaking curve fooled Danny completely and it rolled back to the fence. He put the mitt down.

"How about coming over to a practice game this afternoon?" he asked George, trying not to appear overanxious. "You can pitch for the second team, and we'll see how you make out against the varsity."

George smiled his slow, indulgent smile. "You fellows'll be lucky if you get a hit," he announced as he strode away.

"Hm," said Danny. "Seems to be suffering from a lack of self-confidence."

"What's the difference?" said Gabby. "He'll set the batters on their ears. We won't lose a game with George blazing 'em in!"

However, Danny was worried as he walked home. Coach Payne, who would be back after spring vacation, was a strict disciplinarian. He stood for no nonsense from the squad. A few conceited quips from George might cause Coach . . . Then Danny shook his head. No use worrying before anything happened. For the rest of the week he'd be in charge of practice, and in that time he'd have that giant in line one way or another!

That afternoon he received his first setback. George refused to chase flies in the outfield with the rest of the pitchers and outfielders.

"But Coach Payne insists that our pitchers get their legs in shape by chasing flies," protested Danny.

George good-naturedly flexed his right arm. "Never worry about my legs," he declared. "My arm is the only thing that has to be right. And, brother, you'll find out if it is, real soon."

And Danny did.

George goose-egged the varsity in the five-inning practice game. They were lucky to get two scratch singles. Danny fanned the three times he was up. The ball appeared as big as a white pea as it blazed and darted toward the plate.

"Whee!" chortled Tom. "This guy is better than anything I dreamed of. Wait'll Northwood gets a load of his fast ball!"

"All right, fellows," ordered Danny. "Three laps around the field, then showers."

George stared at him, then started walking slowly for the clubhouse.

"Three laps!" barked Danny.

"I heard you," smiled the giant. "But I'm not taking 'em. I'm a chucker — not a track man."

Danny sat down dejectedly on the bench as the team crowded around him.

Danny suddenly motioned for silence. "Listen, gang," he cried. "We need George pitching for us, but you know as well as I do that he won't last five minutes when Coach comes back Monday."

"I know," groaned Gabby. "One exhibition like this and he's through!"

"I'd like to bust him one!" snapped Tom, clenching his fists.

Danny smiled. "Forget that stuff. George could take us all over without breathing too hard. He's as powerful as an ox."

"What's the answer then?" groaned Gabby.

"I don't know," said Danny seriously. "We've got to pin his ears back somehow. I'll arrange a nine-inning game, with George pitching for the scrubs again."

The next afternoon the Webster ball park was crowded. The news about George's pitching had spread through the grapevine, and it seemed that the entire school was out to see the new sensation. George didn't disappoint the fans. His fast ball was blazing, and his curves were snapping and darting. In fact, it was soon evident that young Jack Brady, the scrub catcher, couldn't hold onto the big fellow's offerings without running the risk of being hurt. Much against his will, Danny had to switch Gabby to catch for the scrubs.

George held the varsity helpless for the first eight innings. The only men to get on base were put there by two errors and a walk. Meanwhile the scrubs, although weak at bat, managed to squeeze a run across on a walk to Gabby and a lusty double by George. The one run loomed large as the varsity came to bat in the bottom of the ninth. Danny tried desperately to rally his men, but they seemed discouraged. Tom was disconsolate.

Suddenly Danny sat up and struck his forehead with his open hand. "Wait!" he cried. "I've got it! Why didn't I think of it before? It's certainly worth a try." He ran over and whispered something in the lead-off batter's ear. Jim Clayton nodded.

George, standing on the rubber, smiled his lazy smile. "Secret orders won't help," he called out.

Clayton swung hard on a sharp-breaking curve and missed by a foot. Then he suddenly bunted the next pitch down the third-base line. George lumbered clumsily off the hill, but Clayton, being fast, easily beat the throw to first for the varsity's initial hit.

Danny pounded Tommy on the back. "It's up to you, boy. The same thing. Get Jim down to second!"

Tommy faked a wild swing, took a high one for a ball, then bunted down the first-base line. George, annoyed, scrambled over and tried to pick up the ball. In his anxiety he slipped and fell. Both runners were safe. Danny was jubilant — a chink in the armor at last!

The next batter bunted to the right of the mound. George just managed to throw him out by an eyelash.

The big fellow, breathing hard from his unaccustomed running, called time out.

"What're we playing," he roared, "patty cakes? Swing at the ball like men — don't pat at it!"

This time it was Danny who smiled indulgently. "What's the matter, big boy — your legs bothering you? You look awfully slow and clumsy out there."

Danny walked up to the plate, trying to ignore the butterflies in his stomach. He gasped as the angry George uncorked the fastest pitch of the game. Danny blinked his eyes and attempted to bunt the blazing ball. But he only got a piece of it and fouled it off. He let two sharp-breaking curves go by for two balls. Then he took an obvious bunting stance at the plate.

"Every day isn't a holiday!" shouted George as he delivered a blazer and ran off the rubber to field the bunt he was sure was coming. But at the last instant Danny switched his grip to the end of the bat and swung hard. Danny's butterflies did flip-flops as he connected squarely and the ball shot on a line toward the onrushing pitcher. George threw up his glove in self-defense, but only partially deflected the liner. The ball hit George on the forehead and bounced into short center! Two runs came scampering in as George was ruefully rubbing the large lump on his forehead.

Danny rushed over to George. "Are you hurt?" he asked anxiously.

"Naw," said George despondently. "Lucky it only skinned me, but it lost me the ball game. That's what hurts!"

Danny took a deep breath. This was it. Coach Payne would be back on Monday, and Danny had to know. "All right," he roared. "Everybody on both teams take three laps. Get the old legs in shape."

He watched George carefully as the boys began jogging around the field. Then he felt his muscles tighten as George started walking slowly for the clubhouse.

Suddenly Danny's heart began hammering as George hesitated and then began jogging after the boys. Tom and Gabby jumped on Danny and hugged him as George began overhauling the squad with his gigantic stride.

"What made you switch from bunting to slugging?" gasped Tom.

"I'll tell you," laughed Danny. "After I signaled Gabby and the scrub infielders to let George handle all the bunts, I still wasn't satisfied. I decided we had to teach the big fellow a further lesson."

They were still laughing when George finished his workout — a whole lap ahead of the rest of the team!

Canoe Race

by Joseph Olgin

As Garry Mason sat in the stern of the White team's number one canoe, he felt very tense and nervous. This was it — the final event of the competition at Camp Pine Wood. The two-mile canoe race — across the lake and back. All through the week the Whites and the Blues had struggled for supremacy. It had been a close, bitter contest with first one team forging into the lead and then the other. Now with all the events but one over, the score was practically even. The Blue team, which Tommy Scott captained, had a slim one-point lead. The canoe race counted for five points — winner take all!

Garry gripped his paddle tightly. Why, oh why, did Joe, the head counselor, take so much time in starting the race off? Garry glanced over at Tommy Scott, captain of the Blues' team, seated in their number one canoe. Tom's face was set and he stared straight ahead. Then Tom turned and whispered something to Burt Johnson, who was piloting the Blues' number two canoe, which occupied the number three lane to the right of Garry. Burt nodded his head in acquiescence.

"I wonder what they're talking about," whispered Garry to Frank Cowen, who was sitting in the White team's number two canoe in the lane to Garry's left.

"I don't know, but we'll have to watch out," muttered Frank. "Tom and Burt are up to something."

Garry forced himself to smile in spite of his inward uneasiness. "Don't worry, Frank," he said. "We'll be ready for any trick they might pull."

He didn't feel as confident as he sounded. The canoe race had been won in the past years by every conceivable trick.

There were four canoes entered in the race. But only Garry and Tom Scott had a chance to win. They were far too experienced paddlers for either of the number two canoes to match them. But even a canoe out of a race could block off a winning canoe or accidentally run into one. The luck of the draw had placed Garry alongside of Burt Johnson. Burt sat confidently and at ease in his trim craft.

Garry knew that the stocky, burly Burt was capable of trying anything. This was Burt's first year in Camp

Pine Wood, and probably his last. You really couldn't pin anything on him, but Burt was suspected of doing anything to win.

Garry licked his lips nervously. Well, he'd keep his eyes open. His main adversary was still Tom Scott. There wasn't much to choose between Tom and himself, and if the White team was to win he had his work cut out for him.

Suddenly Garry was snapped out of his reverie by Joe's sharp directions.

"Remember, the race is to the other side of the lake and back. Any canoe that doesn't actually touch Thompson's dock on the other side will be disqualified. Mr. Sheridan and I will be waiting there in the speedboat to see that you fellows don't foul. White canoe number one, ready?"

"Ready!"

"Blue canoe number one, ready?"

"Ready!"

"Number two canoes, ready?"

"Ready!"

The roar of the gun shattered the late afternoon air and the paddles bit into the water. In no time at all the contestants were well out on the lake, with the cries of the spectators gradually growing fainter. It was one mile across and one mile back, a grueling grind. Garry bent to his task methodically. His paddle flashed in and out of the water with a near-perfect rhythm that it had taken him many summers to master.

He looked over at the other canoes. They were all

about even. "This won't do," he thought, and dug in. His paddle bit deeper into the clear blue water and Garry felt his canoe leap ahead. But the number one Blue canoe leaped ahead with him. In spite of anything they could do, the number two canoes of each team began to lag behind.

A wave of exhilaration shot through Garry. At least he was clear of Burt's canoe. He had been afraid of Burt's ramming into him, or in some other way forcing him out of the race.

"I still have to pass him on the way coming back," thought Garry, "but I'll worry about that when I come to it."

The roar of the speedboat carrying Joe and Mr. Sheridan, the director, over to Thompson's dock interrupted Garry's thoughts for a moment. Then he glanced swiftly at Tom's canoe. It really was traveling! Garry dug in desperately, but in spite of all his efforts the Blue canoe led him by a length. But Garry didn't get discouraged easily. He raised his stroke.

Soon the terrific strain began to tell on him. His muscles ached and he found it hard to breathe. But the two months of hard training had not been wasted. Gradually he crept up and passed Tom's canoe. He reached Thompson's dock two lengths in the lead. The occupants of the speedboat watched him carefully as he touched, then pushed off. In his anxiety to increase his lead, Garry missed a stroke and lost a length of his hard-won advantage as Tom quickly took advantage of Garry's mishap. It was nip and tuck as they started back.

Garry raised his stroke again. He had to win this race —he absolutely had to! Tom and he were practically even in all the camping competitions. The winner of this canoe race would certainly be picked for the best all-around camper. That would mean a scholarship to Camp Pine Wood for next year as a counselor-in-training. Garry gritted his teeth and bore down. His canoe fairly leaped ahead as he put every muscle in his strong back behind his paddle.

Little by little he drew farther ahead and away from Tom Scott's canoe. Garry was beside himself with joy. A scholarship to Pine Wood! If he didn't get it, he wouldn't be able to come back next year. His father hadn't been doing so well and this was to be Garry's last year at camp. But now he'd always be able to go to Pine Wood. A counselor-in-training scholarship would lead to a regular counselor's job — Garry's dream.

"Got him by three lengths," he muttered joyfully. "He'll never catch me now!" The torture in his lungs suddenly eased up as he began to get his second wind. His lips began to move, "Please, please, let nothing happen to me now — a broken paddle or a stitch in the side — or anything." He and the entire White team had worked so hard that they truly deserved this victory.

A few seconds later he passed the White number two canoe just coming up. Frank screamed at him, "Keep plugging, Garry boy, and we're in!"

And Garry did plug! As though his life depended on it, he paddled with every ounce of strength in his body. He was leading by four lengths now.

Suddenly the Blue's number two canoe loomed up ahead of him hopelessly out of the race. Garry immediately noticed something was wrong. Burt was slumped in his seat, not paddling, and writhing with pain.

"Must have a stitch in his side," thought Garry frantically. "His canoe is out of control. I'll have to be careful to go around it."

Burt suddenly slumped over the side of his canoe half in the water and half out. He grasped his side as though he were in great pain. Garry frantically looked for the speedboat, but Joe and Mr. Sheridan were a third of a mile back on Thompson's dock.

"I mustn't stop," thought Garry. "It's a trick. There's nothing wrong with Burt. It's a scheme of his to let Tom win the race." He was about to shoot past when Burt writhed violently and slumped even farther over the side of his canoe. The canoe rocked for a moment, then suddenly turned over, throwing its occupant into the water.

Garry groaned and stabbed his paddle into the water, which brought him to an abrupt stop. If Burt was on the level, he had to stop, otherwise the boy might drown before the speedboat came up. He began to backpaddle as Tom Scott's canoe shot past him without stopping. Garry felt a hot flush of indignation. This *must* be a trick — something Tom and Burt had cooked up between them. Otherwise, why didn't Tom stop?

There was still time to catch up to Tom and pass him. Surely if Tom hadn't known it was a trick he would have stopped. But all this reasoning was of no use. Garry knew what he had to do. His eyes frantically searched the water for signs of Burt. Then he saw Burt come to the surface, floundering desperately. He certainly seemed to be in trouble. If he was faking, he was doing it perfectly.

Without hesitating, Garry leaped overboard, almost upsetting his own canoe. A few strong strokes and he had Burt in a cross-chest carry. He towed him over to his own canoe, where he hung desperately with one hand while he supported Burt with the other.

Burt tried to gasp his thanks.

"Don't try to talk, Burt," Garry said. "You'll be all right. Just lie still. A stitch is painful but not serious. It'll wear off in a little while."

Suddenly a faint cheer rolled across the lake. It came from the assembled Blue team on the dock. They had seen their number one canoe coming in all alone!

The winner and new champion of the competition was Tom Scott. And Garry, captain of the Whites, was out in the middle of the lake, holding onto a canoe with one hand — all his dreams blasted.

Garry's eyes suddenly filled. Then through the mist he saw Joe and Mr. Sheridan come roaring up in their speedboat. Strong arms lifted both boys into the boat.

Joe gripped Garry's hand strongly when he found out what happened. "You're a real Pine Wood man, Garry," he said quietly. "I'm proud of you! Burt's okay now, but if it weren't for you — " Joe didn't finish the sentence.

Mr. Sheridan didn't say anything at all.

The next night, the last of the camp season, the annual banquet was held. Garry sat quietly with his defeated White team and watched the victorious Blues receive their victory banner. Then came the award everyone was waiting for — the best all-around camper! He found it hard to breathe as Joe stepped forward to make the announcement.

"The one who has the most points, and who is therefore the winner of the best all-around camper award, is Tom Scott!"

A deafening cheer rose from the assembled campers and counselors. Tom was popular all right. Garry's heart sank. He had been a fool to hope. In this life only winning performances counted.

Then Mr. Sheridan stepped forward and began to speak. Garry was not listening. He was thinking that this was his last banquet at Pine Wood. Six happy summers here, and now it was over — for good.

He suddenly realized that a hush had fallen over the crowded dining room. Then as though from a great distance he heard Mr. Sheridan's voice.

"And knowing all that he was forfeiting, he deliberately dropped out of the race because a fellow camper was in danger. By doing this, he saved Burt's life."

Garry's heart began to pound wildly. Mr. Sheridan was talking about *him!*

Mr. Sheridan motioned Garry to come to the platform. Then, with his arm around Garry's shoulder, he said, "And therefore I give to Garry Mason a special award — full counselor rank at Camp Pine Wood for as long as he may care to come here."

Mothers' Football Club

by Joseph Olgin

P<small>HIL</small> B<small>RYANT</small> took a quick step forward, adjusted the football in his hands, and swung his powerful right leg upward as hard as he could. There was a loud boom as leather toe met pigskin, and the ball took off in a high twisting arc. Almost everyone on the football field stopped what he was doing and stared.

"I can't believe it," gasped Cliff Jackson as his eyes followed the ball until it hit the ground. Husky Cliff was captain and right tackle of Linwood High's football team. "That punt traveled sixty yards if it went an inch!"

"This is it," yelled Ed Parker, the snappy little quarterback. "Whoever kicked that can used his leg power to drive. He's the smashing left halfback we've been dreaming of. He'll give us the *championship!*"

Cliff and Ed covered the fifty-yard distance to Phil in record time. "W-what school did you come from? W-what position do you play? How fast are you? Can you cut off tackle? How? When? Where?" The questions tumbled over each other before Phil could even answer one.

"Wait a minute," Cliff suddenly laughed. "Let's give the poor guy a chance." He extended his hand. "I'm Cliff Jackson. What's your name?"

"I'm Phil Bryant," said the big blond six-footer. "I'm a transfer from Calvin High."

"What position are you out for?" asked Ed trying to hide the excitement in his voice. "Left halfback?"

"Well," said Phil uneasily. "I — I guess — "

"Enough questions," yelled Cliff. "I'm calling a team race. Then we'll know the answer to the sixty-four-dollar question. Over here, gang. Coach has been delayed a little, so we're having a race to see if there are any speed boys in the club."

Cliff lined up the squad across the field on the goal line. Then he instructed Ed to stand at the other end of the field and pick the winner. As the boys stood straining on the line, Cliff fingered the stop watch.

"On your mark, get set, go!"

The squad broke out fast. Joe Riley, the team's left

half, jumped into an early lead, but Phil Bryant swept by Joe easily at the forty-yard mark and breezed in, the winner by nearly five yards.

Cliff stared at his stop watch overjoyed. "Ten-seven," he gasped. "Our worries are over! With that speed and that weight, who can stop him?"

Cliff sent the squad back to warm up, and he and Ed called Phil aside. "How many touchdowns did you score at Calvin High last year?" they asked.

"Well," said Phil uneasily. "I — er — a — "

"Don't be modest," laughed Cliff. "Listen, how are you at hitting the line? Or do you specialize in end runs? Can you pass?"

Phil didn't answer for a long moment. Then he blurted out. "I — I don't carry at all! I just kick!"

"Don't tell me they've been wasting your talents," cried Ed. "I know you can rock 'em and sock 'em, but we'll change all that. We need touchdowns!"

Phil's face grew red with embarrassment. "I only specialize in kicking. I — I don't carry or play on the defense. I told Coach Connors that when I went out for the team!"

Cliff and Ed suddenly stared at Phil suspiciously. "Why?" they both demanded. "What's wrong? Are you hurt? or — "

Phil suddenly grew angry. "Listen," he cried. "I'm here to practice punting — not to undergo the third degree. Don't bother me with so many questions."

Cliff and Ed made a beeline for Coach Connor's office.

"What gives with that big punting phenom?" they asked. "Is he scared, or what?"

Coach Connors thought for a while, then he answered seriously. "No, boys. Phil's not afraid. It's only that his mother refused to sign the consent slip unless I agreed to use him for kicking exclusively."

"What's she afraid of? Phil's big enough to take care of himself. He's even bigger than Cliff. What a build!"

"I know," said Coach. "But Phil's mother is a widow and Phil is all she has in the world, so — "

"We'll go over and see her," cried Cliff. "We need another good back like a duck needs water."

"It's no use, boys, I tried," repeated Coach. "Don't ask her again. I don't want to embarrass Phil any further. Besides, you have to admire a boy who's willing to give up all the glory to accede to his mother's wishes."

But in spite of Coach's warning, the team did embarrass Phil at every opportunity. Phil was a terrific punter, and although he got Linwood out of many tough spots with his booming kicks, his popularity was zero with the gang!

"Here comes Mamma's boy. Be careful, don't bump into little Phil, he's so fragile!"

Phil never answered the jibes, but many times he bit his lip until it bled.

Linwood had a good season despite the lack of a climax runner, and they came down to the final game with Wilson High with only two losses in eight games. Wilson had the same 6-2 record, and the traditional game was for the league title.

"If we only had Phil running in there," muttered Ed to Cliff the night before the big game.

"We'll get along without the big baby," said Cliff.

"Not now," groaned Ed. "Coach just got the doctor's report on Joe Riley's ankle."

"Don't tell me Joe's out of the game?" said Cliff. "He's our only dependable ball carrier."

"Well, he's not exactly out, but his ankle's in bad shape. If only we could think of a way to get Phil in. He'd be terrific. In the last team race he won by ten yards."

"I know," Cliff banged his fist angrily into his palm. "Here we have the biggest and fastest back in Linwood's history, and he might as well not be on the team for all the good he does us on the offense."

"I've got an idea," said Ed suddenly. "I'm inviting Phil's mother to the game. Phil told me she's never been to one. Maybe once she sees — "

"She won't come," interrupted Cliff.

"Yes she will," cried Ed. "I'll invite all the mothers of the team. Yours, mine, everybody's — down to the last substitute. They'll all come if we put it that way — a Mothers' Football Club!"

The next day the stadium was jammed to capacity. A special box near the fifty-yard line was reserved for the mothers, and they came one hundred per cent strong.

The game was tough and bruising, with neither team

able to gain much ground. At the half, Ed and Cliff, shaking inwardly, tested the results of their experiment. They asked Mrs. Bryant to let Phil carry, but she quietly refused.

"I'm sorry, boys," she said. "But I'm sure you'll win the game anyway."

"We're sunk now!" cried Cliff as the boys turned away. "Joe Riley's ankle won't last this quarter."

And sure enough the doctor wouldn't let Joe continue after the third period. Little Al Ernest filled in for Joe, but he was too small to get anywhere. Phil, whenever called on to punt, did a magnificent job. His booming, twisting kicks kept Wilson at bay, but the crowd never cheered him. They resented his not being in on the attack.

Finally, with only minutes to go, Linwood was forced back to their own seven with the ball in their possession. Fourth down — eighteen yards to go.

Phil was rushed in to punt out of danger. "Block that kick! Block that kick!" roared the Wilson stands.

Phil stood behind his goal line waiting for the ball. The snap back was a little high and the Wilson line charged in like madmen. As Phil hurried to get his kick away, a big Wilson end leaped high in the air and blocked the punt. The ball rebounded straight into Phil's hands. Astonished, Phil grabbed it, hesitated for a moment and then suddenly took off for the sidelines like a frightened deer. He almost knocked a tackler off the field with a savage straight-arm on the ten. He whirled and twisted like a dervish and tore loose from two others at the twenty. At the thirty he was all alone streaking like a runaway express.

The Linwood crowd went berserk. Even the mothers went wild. They threw their arms around each other and screamed as Phil went over the goal line standing up!

Phil seemed strangely worried as he dressed and left the locker room with Cliff and Ed. His mother was waiting for him at the head of the stairs.

"I'm sorry, Mother," said Phil, "but — "

"Sorry," she shouted. "Listen, son, if you hadn't run that ball back, I'd have boxed your ears, big as you are!"

Then they all laughed. "And by the way," boasted Mrs. Bryant, "I've just been elected president of the Mothers' Football Club. Wait till next year — with Phil playing left half we'll win every game on the schedule!"

Kid Brother

by B. J. Chute

TERRY BURTON made a quick pivot, throwing the substitute guard off balance, and hooked a clean shot toward the basket. The ball ripped through the net, and the guard, who had a philosophical nature, said, "Very neat," in an admiring voice.

Terry shrugged. He had learned that maneuver from watching his brother, and it sometimes came in handy. Not that he could shoot with Mac's incredible machine-gun accuracy. Players like Mac Burton turned up only once in a decade, and his name was still magic at Duncan High. Six-letter man. All-State gridiron great, hockey and swimming star, record-breaking shot-putter, captain of the baseball nine, and the spark plug of a championship basketball team. When Mac graduated, Duncan had closed its greatest athletic era.

The two brothers weren't much alike. Mac was big, easy, and spectacular. Terry was slight and strung on wires, a scrub on the football team, not husky enough for hockey. At basketball and tennis he was pretty good — fast and nervous — but not like Mac, who could slice up a defense like a hot knife cutting into butter. You couldn't expect more than one Mac to a family.

Terry sighed inwardly, looking for someone to pass to. He saw that his running mate, Suds Kelly, was on a busy line and elected to try a long one. The ball traveled to the hoop like a needle on a magnet, and it was another goal for the varsity.

The coach blew his whistle and stopped the play to speak to one of the second-team guards. Suds wandered over to retrieve the ball and came back to Terry with it cradled under his arm. "Very handsome bit of shooting," he said approvingly. "You know, Terry, you're looking pretty good this season. Maybe you're wearing Mac's shoes."

Terry laughed and took the ball. "Not me."

"I don't know," said Suds. "You've done plenty of scoring the last few games."

Terry sighted the basket and tossed a free throw in neatly. "Why all the bookkeeping, Suds? I didn't know you were the mathematical type."

"I'm not. I just happened to be looking at the conference scoring records."

"Oh?"

Suds nodded. "Wilder at Conover and Speed Lewis at Washington are out front, but you're crowding them."

Terry, starting over to collect the ball, stopped in his tracks. "Me?" he said incredulously. "You're kidding."

"I mean it. You're as much in line for the *Daily News* cup as any guy in the Conference."

Terry stared.

"You've been averaging nice and high every game," said Suds. "What's the matter? Don't you like cups?"

Terry's heart gave a bound. Three years ago the newspaper cup that was awarded annually to the high scorer of the Little Ten had been won by Mac Burton without a struggle. It was sitting right on the Burton mantelpiece this minute, along with a flock of other trophies. The twin of that, with Terry's name engraved on it, would look pretty nice over the fireplace.

Pretty nice? It would look beautiful. And it would be something to make Mac really proud of his kid brother. He had a sudden vision of bringing that cup home, and of the pride in Mac's eyes. Then he told himself to relax. It was just a dream.

But it was a nice dream. "You sure about the scores, Suds?"

"Sure, I'm sure."

"I never even thought about — " The coach's voice interrupted him, and he went after the ball.

For the rest of that practice he played over his head and kept the subs in hot water. Even the coach whistled gently over a one-hander that went for mileage, and Terry began to think that maybe the cup wasn't just a dream. He could move up fast on Joe Wilder and Speed Lewis if things broke right.

The coach said finally, "Okay, kids, get to the showers. Nice shooting, Terry."

Terry, knee-deep in clouds, followed the gang to the locker room.

The Allison game was slated as a breather, but Terry pointed for it as if it were the season's biggest show. In the pocket of his sweat shirt he carried a list with three names on it. Number one was Joe Wilder — 124 points. Number two was Speed Lewis — 119. Number three was Terry Burton with 114. Both Wilder and Lewis had tough competition to face that afternoon, which might cut down their scoring. Here was where Terry Burton was going to narrow the gap.

He started right in, caging a rebound, before the Allison defense got set. That was two points. Five seconds later he bounced one in from midcourt, and that was four points. Allison began to get attentive, and their lanky center snared an under-the-basket try. Jim Clark at guard put the ball in play again, passing to Suds, who whirled and shot for the basket. The ball wandered around the rim, and finally dropped through.

That was six points for Duncan, but only four for Terry. The next time the ball came his way, he was up the floor and Suds was near the free-throw line. Terry hesitated, sighted the basket and shot. The ball hit the backboard and bounced out.

Suds looked disappointed. Terry said, "Darn it," under his breath. A moment later, however, he was awarded a free throw and skipped the ball right into the basket. That was five points toward the chance to shine up the high scorer's cup.

Duncan pulled out at the half on the long end of a 29-24 score, but Suds was edgy. "We ought to have a lot more points on them by now. What's the trouble with us?"

Terry said calmly, "We're doing all right." They were, too, and he should know. Twelve of those 29 points he had scored personally, and there was still half the game to go. If Wilder and Lewis were being bottled up at all that afternoon in their own games, Terry's scoring would make a nice jump ahead. He wasn't going to mention it at home, though. He was saving his news until the day when he could put the cup — his own cup, the first Mac Burton's kid brother had ever won — into Mac's hands.

"Relax, Suds," he said.

Time was in again, and Duncan opened up with a free-shooting exhibition starring Terry Burton. They didn't all go in, but he was playing percentages and didn't expect a ringer every time. The Duncan offense didn't seem as highly coordinated as it had in some games, but it clicked, and when the final gun went off Allison was trailing eight points, and Terry had hung up a record for himself of eight goals and five free throws. That added up to 21 points.

He whooped off to the locker room in high spirits and tracked down the team manager who was a walking encyclopedia of information. "Hey — Jimmy!"

"Yup?" Jimmy, sorting equipment, lost count but stayed amiable.

"Do you know how the Conover and Washington games came out?"

"Uh — Conover took Jefferson 72-70. And Washington was leading by three points, last I heard."

"Wilder and Lewis doing much scoring?"

"Pretty good. Wilder picked up 19, and I think Speed Lewis got 17. Why?"

"Nothing." Evidently no one but Suds had noticed how the scoring was shaping up. It was too early in the season for most of the guys to think much about it. Feeling good, Terry free-wheeled over to Suds. "Conover and Washington both won their games," he announced.

Suds glanced up. "Not bad. Their competition was really tough. Terry, we ought to have won by more than eight points. That didn't look so good against a team like Allison. They're in the Conference basement."

Terry grunted and reached for his sweat shirt, diving into the pocket for his slip of paper and beginning to figure. "Wilder 19 more points. And 17 for Lewis. And I got 21. That's — " He fell into a mathematical trance, then grinned. "Gee, another good break like today's game, and I'll be in the lead."

Suds gave him a sharp sideways look. Terry went on eagerly studying his precious slip of paper.

It was turning into a pretty good season for Duncan. They won and lost their share, but they stayed in the top brackets. Terry stayed in the top brackets too, sometimes ahead and sometimes behind Wilder and Lewis, but always elbowing them. Each game brought the dream of possessing the cup a little closer to coming true.

On the afternoon they shellacked Fenwick Prep, Terry rode high on a wave of confidence and a scoring collection of 20 points. Unfortunately, that was the afternoon Joe Wilder, doing some collecting himself, set a scoring high by plunking 12 goals and four free throws through the net.

Terry got that bit of news on his way home from the game, and his heart took an elevator ride to the cellar. He could lose the cup easy, and with it his one chance to do something in sports that would make his brother really proud. He sloshed along through melting snow, hands jammed in pockets, and thought about Joe Wilder and Conover High. Duncan would face Conover in its last game of the season, and Terry had envisioned himself outpointing and outfighting his nearest rival. But right now he was trailing Wilder in the scoring, and there might not be a contest at all. Come the last game, Joe Wilder might be sitting right inside the cup, defying all comers.

Up to now Terry had been thinking only in terms of winning the cup, seeing his brother's excitement and pride. Now he started to think in terms of losing it, and he didn't like the picture.

Someone behind him yelled, "Hey, Terry!" and he turned to find Suds splashing through a puddle. He waited. Suds was a consoling guy.

"You big dodo," said Suds good-temperedly, "I thought you were going to meet me outside the gym."

"I'm sorry. I went over to the Center to find out how Joe Wilder did this afternoon."

"That was a foregone conclusion," Suds grumbled. "Conover won hands down. Must have."

"Yeah. But Joe Wilder scored 28 points."

Suds whistled. "Nice work if you can do it. He really went to town."

"It puts him in the lead," Terry said shortly.

There was a rather long silence. Then Suds said, "For the high-scorer's cup, you mean?"

"Naturally."

There was another dragged-out pause. "Uh — Terry."

"Yup?"

Suds looked slightly embarrassed. "Look, pal, I don't want to stick my oar in, but aren't you thinking too much about that cup? I mean, just lately you seem to care more about your own scoring board than about the team. I — " He trailed off, as Terry stared at him in astonishment, then he tried again. "Well, look at the game this afternoon, Terry. We set up feeder plays with me in close, and then you shot from midcourt."

"I made them, didn't I?"

"Yes, but that's not the point. Gee, Terry, nobody'd be more pleased than me if you won the cup, but heck, it isn't that important."

Not important? The silver cup that Mac Burton had won, and that his kid brother was hoping to win after him? Not important, the chance to make Mac really proud of him?

He started to retort, then shrugged. You couldn't expect anyone else to understand what it meant. Suds, naturally, was thinking about the team. Well, that was what Terry was thinking about too — a team that won on points. Terry was going to make those points personally, that was all. Nobody could complain about that.

He said good night to Suds at the corner and went on home, thinking about the cup.

The afternoon of the big Conover game found Terry in an advanced state of nerves. Normally he took a game in his stride, but this was different. This game was the payoff, and it would make or break his chances. Speed Lewis was out of the running for the cup, after a week's layoff because of a sprained ankle. Joe Wilder had hit a short slump. Terry, playing the percentages, shooting for his basket whenever he laid his hands on the ball, had pulled up nearly level.

With one game to go, Joe Wilder stood at 230 points. Terry had 226. The Conover-Duncan game would bring them together and decide the cup winner.

In the locker room, he sat on the bench and drew deep breaths, trying to steady his pulse. The way he felt now, he almost wished he hadn't asked Mac to come, but his desire to have Mac share his triumph had got the best of him. And Mac had cut a class at the university to be there in the cheering section.

Terry swallowed hard.

The coach said, "All right, kids, get going," and the squad jumped to their feet, pushing through the doorway, anxious for action. The Duncan rooters started yelling as soon as they came out on the floor, and the gay-bannered gymnasium thundered with cheers.

Terry spotted Mac in the gallery and waved to him with a hand that felt as stiff as a poker, then he put his attention on the court.

The Conover squad was passing the ball around in a snappy drill, and Terry took a good look at Joe Wilder. Tall, loose-built, and easy-moving, he had nice coordination and a sharp eye for the basket. Terry found himself wondering if Joe's mind was fastened on the cup too. Then the referee signaled time, and Terry jerked his attention back to the moment.

"Shorty" Long, Duncan's storklike center, took the opening tap-off, and Tony d'Esta picked it up to short-pass to Terry. Terry, finding he had a Conover guard wrapped around his neck, pivoted, feinted to Suds, and then broke for the basket in a fast dribble. His guard was made of glue, and Terry's shot for the basket was rushed. The ball hit the rim and ricocheted wildly.

Joe Wilder drove in, picked it up, and stampeded for his own fireside. He ducked a guard, passed, took the pass back again on a quick exchange that had shaken him loose and shot for the basket from a good angle.

The ball dropped through, and the Conover stands roared and stamped.

Terry frowned. Two more points for Joe. That was six now he had to make up. The ball was thrown in, and Conover broke up a pass and brought it into the danger zone again. This time the try was short, and Suds collected off the backboard.

Terry's fingers yearned for the ball. Suds whirled, broke, looked as though he was planning a long one, and then saw Terry in a cozy set-up play under the basket. He passed to Tony, and Tony beamed it to Terry.

Good guys! Terry flicked the ball through the hoop, special delivery.

Conover and Duncan settled down to business. Both teams played a fast-breaking offensive game, long pass and short pass. Duncan normally varied this with a cagey ability to fall into a set formation when the steam-roller offense jammed, but this afternoon Terry Burton was spearheading the attack, and Terry was driving for the basket. In the first quarter the percentages rode with him, and every opening he saw for a goal he filled.

When the period ended, Duncan had 17 points to Conover's 14, and it was largely due to Mac Burton's kid brother. Terry, one eye on the basket and one on the cup, had two columns of figures in his mind. One was the score. The other was his own scoring average. For the first time that season he had an edge on Joe Wilder. He was going to hold that edge.

Play in the second quarter was fast and tough. A long-legged Conover obstacle named Anderson had inherited the job of playing bodyguard to Terry, and trouble developed. Anderson was allergic to long tries for the goal and he did everything but put a handcuff on Duncan's ace forward. Terry, goal-conscious, tried to drive around Anderson near the side line and was awarded a free throw. Terry made it good, and piously hoped that Anderson would relax his earnest attention to duty.

Anderson didn't. He just kept better track of what he was doing with his hands. And Terry, who was in no mood for a free-passing game, clung stubbornly to his personal basket tries; while Conover, in possession of the ball, opened up and passed all over the field. Conover clicked on a rebound and two center-court tries and scrambled into a perilous two-point lead, 28 to 26. Terry still held his own fragile scoring edge, but if Joe Wilder was really opening up, it wouldn't stay around long.

Terry tightened and put on pressure. Every time he dropped one through the hoop, the cup got a little nearer and a little shinier. And up in the stands Mac Burton was watching his kid brother.

Shorty floated a pass, and Terry jockeyed to shake Anderson. It was like shooting through a picket fence, and the hook shot he tried was wide. Suds, in the next time out, caught at Terry's elbow. "You'd better try and get some of those passes down my way, kid. Anderson's doing a Scotch-tape job on you."

Terry shook his head impatiently. Nobody was going to stop him today, Anderson or Suds or anyone else. He was going to connect with enough shots if he had to climb into the basket with them personally. That meant a win both for him and for Duncan. They paid off scores on baskets, didn't they? Baskets were what Duncan needed, and it was going to be Terry Burton who made them.

The half ended with the gallery yelling and whistling when Conover put on a razzle-dazzle exhibition that pulled them ahead to a 34-29 lead. The teams trailed off the floor and headed for the lockers. Suds flopped down beside Terry. "Really tough," he said.

Terry nodded. He was still those two points up on Joe Wilder, but they could go with the wind. Then he realized that Suds, naturally, was thinking about the score, and he had a moment's uneasiness because he hadn't been thinking about it himself. He shook that off. The cup for him and victory for Duncan would be won together.

"We'll take 'em," Terry said confidently.

When the referee poked his head informatively through the doorway, the players pulled themselves to their feet and hitched up their pants. An ear-splitting ovation met them as they ran out on the floor, with the galleries panting for action.

Both teams obliged, opening up with basket bombardments. Conover rolled into high gear with a series of plays that worked three times running before Duncan got wise to the changed tactics and clamped down defensively. Joe had made only one of the goals, but that pulled him even with Terry. When Duncan's ace laid his hands on the ball, the basket loomed so large in his mind that he could have dropped a watermelon through at a hundred yards.

The shot flicked through the net, and the Duncan rooters nearly choked with excitement. Someone let out a yell like a foghorn, and Terry grinned widely. You could spot Mac's cheers a mile away. "Stick around," he thought, "and there'll really be something to cheer for."

A spot opened up a minute later. Terry, positive he couldn't miss, blasted from midcourt. The shot was long on distance but short on luck, and the ball circled the rim and bounded off. Conover 40, Duncan 31.

Play speeded up, racing up and down court, in a wide-open furious battle for points. Terry, charged roughly on a lay-up, converted the double personal and felt a little safer with a four-point lead over Joe Wilder.

The spectators were on their feet half the time, shouting as if lung power could push the ball through the hoop, and the officials pounded the boards, chasing the play. Terry, his lead over Wilder acting like a shot in the arm, began to play way over his head, moving with that peculiar lightness and ease that a player sometimes feels when he is really on. Not every shot scored, but the failures were near misses and beautifully balanced, and he kept hearing his name yelled above the general formless cheering.

The quarter ended with Terry riding high. He accepted a towel from the team manager and rubbed his face, breathing hard. Someone said, "Terry," and he turned around to find Suds at his elbow. Suds' round face was anxious.

"Yup?" said Terry. "We're doing all right, huh?"

"They've got six points on us. What do you mean, we're doing all right?"

It hadn't been exactly the thing to say. Terry tripped over an explanation. "I mean — well, six points isn't — "

Suds' voice had an edge. "I know what you mean," he said sharply. "You mean you're doing all right. You and that cup you're so set on winning."

Terry glanced at Suds with a quick sense of shock. The guy was really sore — Suds, who never got stirred up about anything.

Suds went on. "You're playing percentages, aren't you? You're shooting for the cup, not for the game. I told you what was going to happen."

Terry said defensively, "What do you mean? I've done more scoring for Duncan than anyone else on the team."

"You can say that again," Suds snapped. "You're practically hatching that ball out, the way you stick to it. Whose ball game do you think it is — yours or Duncan's?"

"I don't see what you're so steamed up about," Terry protested uncomfortably.

"You don't, huh?" Suds' voice sharpened. "You're playing percentages, and that's all right. But you're playing them for yourself, not for the team, and if you keep it up we'll lose the game." There was a short silence. "If that's the way you want it, okay. But just take a look at the scoreboard, and be sure you know what you're doing."

He walked off to join the others. Terry stood still, watching him go.

Conover 51, Duncan 45.

They could lose.

He hadn't thought about that before. His mind had

been fixed on two scores, his and Joe Wilder's. He was ahead of Joe now; all he had to do was to hold that lead. Joe had been doing a lot of passing to teammates, setting up shots, so his score had stayed down while Terry's climbed. But at the same time Conover had been pushing ahead of Duncan.

Terry rubbed his chin. He only had to hold his lead for the cup. As long as Joe was playing a five-man game, that lead would stay, even if Terry quit bombing the basket and freezing to the ball. He wanted to win for Duncan. He wanted the cup. He could have both.

When play opened up again, Terry started paying attention to teamwork. A Duncan team that had looked good began to look better. The game was strictly speedway stuff, and the crowd loved it. Hoarse croaks of encouragement testified to voices that had given under the strain. The cheerleaders wound themselves into knots. Even Mac's Comanche howls were lost in the general uproar.

They went into the home stretch, giving everything they had. It was in through the hoop and out through the net for the ball, and the score mounted. That was when Joe Wilder started a bull's-eye routine. His teammates fed him the ball, and he dropped it through. One goal, two goals — Conover and Duncan pulled even on a 66-all standoff with Wilder dropping in the tying count.

That goal did more than tie up the scoreboard. It tied up Joe Wilder and Terry Burton in the race for the cup.

Terry was slow in getting back to the lockers. He was one of a quintet of heroes, and the Duncan rooters had mobbed them, but all the cheering in the world couldn't ease the sharp thrust of his disappointment.

There would be other Conover-Duncan games, but this one had been Terry's only chance for glory. Games would come and go and be forgotten, but that cup would have stayed on the Burton mantelpiece. Nothing could fill the empty space he had mentally saved for it.

He walked into the locker room, pulled off his sweat shirt and flung it down on a bench. Someone said, "Hi, kid."

He turned around. It was Mac. "Nice game," he said. "Really nice."

Terry said, "Yeah." This was to have been the big moment. But the cup on which he had set his heart — the shining proof to Mac that his kid brother really had the stuff — now belonged to Joe Wilder.

There was a short silence, then Mac said, "Suds tells me you were in line for the high-scorer's cup, Terry. You threw it away on that pass, didn't you?"

Terry's shoulders moved resentfully. He wished Suds had kept his mouth shut. He'd rather Mac had never known he had failed. "Thrown it away" was what Mac called it. Well, that was what he had done.

Mac wouldn't have let that happen. Mac would have scored on that last shot; he'd have won both the cup and the game in one sure, brilliant play. That was what being a real athlete meant. They came only one to a family. He wasn't ever going to see the look in Mac's eyes that he had been wanting.

"Kid," said Mac, "I've never been so proud of any guy in my life. That was real ballplaying. The Burtons never turned out a better sport."

Terry stared at him, unbelieving. The look he'd been waiting for was there, and Mac Burton's kid brother was on the receiving end.

"Heck," said Mac. "All a cup adds up to is a lot of silver-polishing."

Terry drew a sudden, deep breath. He knew what Mac meant. The thing he had now wouldn't need any polish. It would stay nice and bright — always.

Pop Can Wear the Medal

by Mary Coleman Jackson

W<small>E WATCHED</small> B<small>OB</small> D<small>OWNEY</small> every day as he put in two sweaty hours jogging around the track like a robot or sprinting like a crazy man. When the rest of us stood joking in the shade of the bleachers on the west end of the field, Coach Markham would growl at us. "Cut it out, you clowns! If every man worked as hard as Downey, we'd be sure to go to the State Finals and *win!*"

Bob would run toward us with his gray track pants flapping loosely about his stringy legs. If it had been me or one of the other guys, someone would have started

clapping or booing or calling out the names of famous
race horses. But we didn't treat Bob that way. The coach
would praise him and we'd listen quietly. Bob would
smile and wipe his face and neck on the sleeve of his
sweat shirt. Then, if his two hours were up, he'd hurry
to the dressing room. We would forget him and put in
a bit more time sprinting, hurdling, and jumping before
the coach or the twilight called us in.

Inside, the other fellows shouted to one another
above the hiss and splash of the showers. They slapped
towels across their backs and thighs, slipped clothes
onto still damp bodies and drifted out into the spring
evening in small groups. I always waited to be the last
to leave the locker room, for there would be no one to
walk with me. There never was, for I am Jackie Murray, a black boy, and as alone on my way home as Bob
Downey was on the field.

My teammates scattered north, south, and west
away from Coolidge High. I was the one who waited
for the eastbound Dayton Avenue bus. Every thirty
minutes this bus travels past new wide-lawned homes
and tiny shops until it crosses River Boulevard. Then it
slows to a crawl, picking up and letting off people like
me who live in the old-fashioned frame houses. I liked
East Dayton Avenue. The men and boys I saw all knew
me and waved. If I whistled or smiled at the girls, they
would giggle and toss their heads. Besides all this, East
Dayton led to home.

Most nights when I opened the door, Mom would
still be cooking and I would talk to Pop before we ate.

He loved to speculate on my chances of beating all the local competition in my events. He bragged as if he thought I was the whole team. I would try to set him straight about Bob being in the quarter-mile as well as me. And about Pete Jenkins in the pole-vault and Ralph Ayers in the 110 high hurdles. If Mom overheard us she'd give a little sniff of disgust. "I thought everyone was worrying about equal chances to learn, not equal chances to run around half-naked," she'd say. "Well, times do change! Come to dinner, you two!"

After dinner, Pop would leave, dressed in the monkey suit he wore to wait table at Waverley's Steak House at the other end of Dayton Avenue. If Mom didn't have a late appointment at her beauty shop, we'd both spread our work on the table. Mom had letters, shop bookkeeping, and household bills. I had homework, especially geometry and senior English. Everything became quiet except for the rustle of papers and the scratching of pencils.

I always intended to study hard, but before long I'd begin to daydream about the team and graduation and things that could happen afterward. Sometimes I'd wonder about the way Mom worked so hard to save for my education, and the way Pop was so hooked on me winning an athletic scholarship to State University. He said he had been a waiter all his life and he wanted me to be a lawyer. But he worried more about my running than he did my studying. He never listened, either, when I talked about other things I'd like to do instead of studying law.

Mom would notice me daydreaming and reach over and tap my hand. I'd study again until my head began to nod and then I'd go to bed. Just before sleep came I'd think about Bob and me and the quarter-mile. We were both good, but I wanted to be the best. I kept a record of Bob's times and tried to stay ahead of them. He was a funny guy. Hard to know and real hard to beat!

The days slipped by — all nearly alike except that the quarter-mile rivalry between Bob and me began to attract attention. Our team won all its meets, and Bob and I helped to pile up the points. Besides the sprinting, Bob was strong in the broad-jump and I was pretty good as a high-jumper. We also ran third and anchor in the four-man mile relay. The coach was pretty pleased with our whole team.

The *Woodsfield Journal* carried a story on us with some interesting statistics. It pointed out that Bob and I were the same age, and the same height, that we varied only seven pounds in weight, and wore the same size shoe. Only Bob was white and I was black. That last fact wasn't in the paper, but it was an important one.

The Monday before our meet with Ruxton Trade High, a reporter *and* a photographer came to our workout. They took shots of Milt Williams in the broad-jump pit and of Ralph taking a hurdle. When they were ready for Bob and me it had gotten cool and the coach told us to dress. The photographer posed us together beside the first trophy Coolidge High had ever won. Then we picked up our books from the bench and hurried home. Midterm exams were coming up and I needed to study. Geometry really worried me; as soon as I got a seat on the bus I opened the book with its green Coolidge High cover. I looked down and got a real surprise. This was a chemistry book. I turned to the fly leaf and saw Bob's name there: Robert Pierce Downey, 113 N. Edgerton Avenue. I'd picked up Bob's chemistry, and he had my geometry book.

I knew I couldn't face the exam unless I studied; I had to have that book. So when the bus braked up to the curb at River Boulevard, I jumped off. In half an hour or so, I could get to North Edgerton, trade books, and be on my way home again.

The bus I took was crowded. I stood stiffly to keep from banging up against anyone as we bounced along. I hadn't traveled this way since I was eight or nine, on my way to trumpet lessons. Then, I would sit down anywhere. Now I was aware of my difference and of how some people felt about it. This awareness tightened my muscles and it was harder than ever to stand without bumping into others. I was so anxious when the bus driver called my stop that I stumbled as I left the bus.

North Edgerton was a street of little houses. Bob's was close to the corner. I walked down the path of cracked bricks that led to a sloping porch. As I lifted my hand to knock on the door, I heard a tapping at the window. Looking that way I saw an old man. He was shaking his head and waving me away. "Go back, boy." His voice came to me clearly. "Don't care what you're selling, we don't want it."

"I'm not selling anything," I called. "Does Bob Downey live here? I've got his book!"

Interest changed the old man's face. He beckoned me to come in. Once inside, I understood more about Bob. This little old man in the wheelchair was his father, and he didn't have any legs. There was a blanket across his lap with nothing under it.

I could see all the house from where I stood, and every bit of it was clean and bare. Spring coldness that had come in the door with me went all about the place without meeting fire heat. The old man was mending a shirt that I had seen Bob wear. He looked me up and down and motioned me to sit down.

"You're tall, aren't you? I don't like people looking down at me, so sit! Bob'll be here soon, I s'pose. Said he wouldn't stay on the job long, 'count of he wants to study." As he talked he held up a needle and began poking a thread at it. His aim was wobbly and I wanted to take over for him as I do for Mom. But I didn't know how he would like it.

I held my breath until the needle was threaded and then let it out all at once. The old man heard me and laughed. "I'll bet you thought I couldn't do it," he said. "You young kids are all alike. Haven't found out you can do whatever you have to do."

He went on with his mending, not one bit embarrassed as my pop would have been. He went on talking too. "You got a book for Bob? How come?"

I told him about our books being on the bench together while we posed for the photographer, and he stopped me right there.

"So you're Jackie Murray! I didn't know you was a colored boy. Bob never mentioned it. Well, well! Right glad to meet you." He took a few stitches. "Wish I could see you running one of them ree-lays with Bob, but I guess I can't."

I sat there without saying much and he kept the conversation going. "Never thought this running would come to anything, but fast as I tell Bob to save his energy for books so's he can get a scholarship to college, he tells me that running and jumping will do the same thing. All I know is, it's got to be books or legs to help him, cause it ain't going to be me. No sirree! This old no-good man can't help Bob one bit!" I guess the little laugh he gave was bitter. "Yep, the boy takes care of the man around here. And does a good job too. I ain't complaining. But he don't get much fun 'cept for that running stuff."

A picture of Bob running and sweating with hardly ever a smile passed through my mind as the old man spoke.

"Surprises you to see me sit here sewing, don't it? Well, it surprises me too. Me sewing, while a boy is out working! I'll bet you feel sorry for yourself sometime. But you shouldn't. You got someone behind you pushing. I can tell by your clothes."

He came to the end of the tear in the shirt and tightened and broke his thread. He held the shirt up and found one more rip. A wide grin spread over his face and he handed me the needle and the spool of thread.

"Well, son," he said. "I saw you working with me before, so this time I'll just let you do it." We both smiled while I threaded the needle. As I handed it back to him, we heard footsteps on the bricks.

"That's Bob! He don't like me to do this," the old man whispered. He folded the shirt, jabbed the needle into it and pushed it beneath the blanket.

Bob stepped in, real surprised to see me. He listened and smiled and we exchanged books. Then there was nothing to say but good-bye. I went out the door and began to trot back to the bus stop. The wind bit into me and I wondered if Bob was going to put some heat on in his house. The smell of cooking rode on the wind and I wondered what Bob was going to give the old man for dinner. Then I wondered about my own dinner.

In twenty minutes I was stepping into our kitchen, sniffing the odor of meatballs, hot biscuits, and the green smell of vegetables. "Wash your hands! Where've you been?" said Mom. Dad slapped me on the back.

"What was your time today, fellow? Did you show that Downey guy the soles of your shoes? Down with Downey!" Pop laughed loud and long and didn't notice that I wasn't laughing.

Later on I told him about the old man at Bob's house. He nodded sympathetically. "Sounds like a good boy. Too bad he can't win. Not against you. Guess he should change to another race."

I always felt funny while Pop was boasting about me and downing other guys. He sounded selfish and kind of dumb. I'd suddenly think, suppose I didn't win? Suppose my times were slow? Suppose I didn't even get a scholarship? Was that so terrible? Mom had my money for college all stashed away. I didn't need things the way Bob needed them. But Pop kept on talking and talking and talking.

Well, I knew I had to study, and I did. And I came through all my exams in good shape. Everyone on the team did. The Friday after exams we won our last league meet and became eligible for the State Finals at Sweetwater.

We were walking on air. The coach tried to bring us all down to earth, but we were too keyed up about the overnight trip and the chance for fame and glory. The *Woodsfield Journal* helped stir us up with write-ups about each one. Of course I saved mine and I saved Bob's, and underlined the sentence that credited Bob with running his quarter-mile relay lap in 47.5 seconds. That's fast. And it meant that his time from a standing start could be fast too.

Early Monday morning something happened that brought *me* down hard! I turned on the radio, *Daybreaker News and Tunes,* and heard that the folks in Sweetwater didn't want me running there. They didn't want a black boy eating and sleeping and running with the white boys in their town. They said it was their civil right *not* to have me if they didn't want me.

I couldn't listen anymore. I just lay there in my bed until Mom stuck her head in the door to tell me how late it was. I bathed and dressed and ate breakfast so Mom wouldn't be able to tell that I felt miserable. I left home, half planning not to go to school at all. But I heard a car approach from behind. I looked back and saw that it was Coach Markham's. He beckoned and opened his car door. When I got in he didn't say anything, just drove pretty fast to school. He parked in the faculty parking lot and led me into the principal's office.

Mr. Houskey jumped up when he saw us. "Jack," he said, "this is a bad thing. But I don't want you to feel too low about it. I'm going to hold an assembly today. Coach Markham and I agreed on what we will say. If you cannot take part in that Sweetwater meet, then no boy from this school will put his foot on that field. Now go to your classes and don't worry. It's not a problem for a boy to deal with." He squeezed my shoulder as he turned me toward the door. With his other hand he waved Coach Markham to a chair.

I walked out alone, and wandered down the hall until I found an open door. I went in and sat down and buried my head in my arms. Now I had a double hurt! Number one; I wasn't wanted. Number two; I would be the cause of the others missing a chance to run in Sweetwater. Even Bob would miss running in a meet that university coaches and scouts would be sure to attend.

I wished there was a hole to crawl in. I wished I had never tried out for the team. I wished I had enrolled at Dunbar High where most of the black kids went. I wished and wished. Funny, though, I never wished I was white, although that would have solved the whole problem.

Finally a teacher came in who had never been very friendly to me. But now she smiled and blushed and told me how awful this thing was. All day long at school everyone else acted the same way and said the same thing.

I had a bad time getting home. People pointed and stared on the west side of River Boulevard. On the east side they crowded around and gave me advice.

Pop was sitting on the porch when I finally reached home. He was so mad that his voice had lost some of its volume.

"Somebody ought to do something about those people in Sweetwater," he groaned. "Somebody needs to put them away, 'cause they all must be crazy. Why, my boy is just as good as most of them and better than some. They're crazy. Plain crazy!" He stopped for breath and this gave me a chance to slip into the house.

Mom saw me standing in the kitchen door and she started filling my plate with some things she knew I liked. "Times like these, you need food you enjoy," she remarked. She put the plate on the table and hugged me. "Why didn't you tell me this morning?" she asked. "Now go wash your hands and eat. I know there's no answer to that question."

I didn't feel hungry but I managed to eat enough to please Mom. She had to force Pop to eat. After each forkful, he'd chew and swallow and grumble some more about the Sweetwater people. There in the kitchen, in between Mom and Pop, things didn't seem so bad. But just as we finished the dishes the doorbell rang. And the telephone. For the rest of the evening it was like the night my grandmother died. People were coming and calling and we even got a telegram. I began to feel bad again.

By the next day it seemed that the whole world knew about me. And I could tell that the fellows on the team were disappointed. I felt that it was all my fault.

"Ain't your fault," Pop shouted when he found out how I was feeling. "Ain't nobody's fault but them old-fashioned, ignorant, backlash folks that live in that little old backward town!"

The week dragged by. Each evening we practiced with more kids in the stands and more grownups watching through the chain-link fence on the north side of the field. I was the big attraction and I felt like a prize boob. I tried to concentrate on beating Bob's time: 47.5 with a running start: a possible 48 flat from the blocks. It was the best way to forget the mess things were in, and Bob was willing to accept any challenge.

I learned, too, that some Sweetwater people were ashamed of what had happened, while there were some Woodsfield people who were glad I had been "put in my place." A few Woodsfield parents tried to force Mr. Houskey to send the team without me, but he stood his ground. Pop came home one night pretty pleased because Tom Linley, the editor of the *Woodsfield Journal* had come to one of his tables to talk about me.

"Linley's a big man in this town," Pop declared loudly. "Runs that paper, trustee in his church, belongs to everything that counts, and tells a whole lot of people what to do! Talked with me about ten minutes. Nice guy. Got his head screwed on real tight!"

Pop was happy, but I was bugged. Everyone was talking about me. How I hated it! I wanted to shout at the world. "Stop talking about me. Stop looking at me. Let the other guys go run and just let me alone!"

Yet on Friday when I came home, Pop was standing in front of our house yelling to his friends across the street. And yelling good news! He grinned when he saw me. "Have you heard?" He punched me in the stomach. "I just got the news. You're in, boy. You're going to that meet and you're going to show your heels to the world!" He followed me into the house and he didn't stop talking until Mom got cross with him.

Exactly a week later the team crowded onto a chartered bus. We had canvas bags packed with pajamas and towels; we had a little extra money in our pockets; and I had an extra muscle in my stomach that kept winding up tight and then spinning loose.

Fifteen minutes away from school the bus hit a superhighway and stepped up to 70 miles an hour. In four hours we were in Sweetwater.

When the meet began on Saturday I was trembly on the inside and sweaty on the outside. It was a bad way to feel if you're supposed to be a key man on a team. I loosened up a bit when the competition started and got a second place in the high jump. But, like I said, I don't remember much about it. All of a sudden it seemed I was standing at the starting line with a low sun at my back so that my shadow was stretching far ahead, dark and thin on the dirt track. Luck had pulled me through trial heats and up to this moment.

This was an important race. The crowd in the stands grew quiet as the announcer's voice came echoing from the public address system, calling the race and giving the names of the seven runners and the schools they represented. He read the total points for all teams in the meet. I knew then that if Bob and I could claim the first two places, Coolidge High would win the meet even without points from the relays.

We were to run this 440 around one turn of the track and the starting line was staggered. I had drawn lane two. Luck, again! Bob was two lanes away on my right. I was glad that neither of us had drawn the choppy inside lane or the outside one that, in a staggered start, set you off ahead so that you seemed to be racing alone. I watched Bob in his kelly green jersey. He was kicking and toeing the track. He's fast, I told myself. Be faster!

Now the judges strolled to their positions and the starter lifted his gun. There were no false starts; the race was on.

Forty-eight seconds! That's good time for a quarter-mile sprint. But today I prayed to run it in less. The first 220 yards I took as hard as I could. I surged ahead of all the striving, leg-driven bodies except one — the one in the green jersey. I was within reach but out of reach; the staggered start and the turn beyond were no help in deciding how great the gap was to be closed. Head down, my mind willing my legs into a smooth oily stride, I went into the turn. Stride — stride — stride — I told myself, and be ready to come out of the curve and hit the straight banging and fighting for the lead. But the green patch stayed ahead as though drawing me along behind. It bobbed and jerked and led me. Bob is tight, I thought. I willed myself to stay loose and burn, burn, burn the fuels of energy and determination that would close the gap between us. I prayed, I strained for the speed to surpass his speed and draw him closer, closer. . . . Then I saw the tape fly.

We passed the judges and slowed our speed and jogged a little farther down the track, stopping together to gasp for breath. The crowd's roar sounded as though someone had turned a giant radio up to full volume. The judges went into a huddle of nodding heads and waving arms. When the public address system began to sputter the crowd sound faded.

"Quiet, please! It was a close one. We're waiting to hear from the judges."

In the silence I could hear my heart beating and Bob's heavy breathing.

"I didn't quite get you," I told him. "I was close, but you hit the tape."

He smiled and shrugged and turned expectantly toward the judges. One stepped away from the huddle and came hustling over. But he passed Bob by and touched me. ME!

I heard Bob suck up air in surprise. I heard the crowd cheering raggedly as the P.A. squawked, "Jackie Murray, Coolidge High, winner; Bob Downey, Coolidge High, second place; Joe Burns, Ruxton Trade High, third place."

"Not me!" I pulled at the judge's arm. "Not me!" He turned away quickly. Someone slapped me on the back.

"Go get your medal, champ!" I was pushed forward toward the judges' box.

I walked there, unwilling, ashamed, and I got there soon enough to hear them arguing.

"It looked like a dead heat to me, but as you say . . ."

"I say the Downey boy came in first, but it's better this way."

"Sure," said the judge who had tapped me, "the Downey boy may have been first, but if we had picked him over that black kid in a close race like this someone would have started screaming!"

Then they noticed me standing there and stopped talking and began to smile.

"Listen!" I said. "I didn't win. Bob did!"

They kept on smiling and hoping that I hadn't heard them and pretending that they hadn't heard me. One pinned the first place medal on my shirt.

I looked for Coach Markham and found him. I caught his arm.

"I didn't win, Coach, Bob did! Not me!"

He looked all over the ground and then in the sky for an answer, but he couldn't find one. He grunted and chewed his lip.

"Come on, Coach. It wasn't fair!"

He moved my hand from his arm gently. "Snap out of it, Murray. You've still got a relay to run. So has

Bob." He walked away, leaving me standing there filled with more of that sick sadness. The kicks had gone out of the track meet again. Yes, I had wanted to win. But I wanted to win fair and square and wear a medal to prove it. But I didn't want a medal pinned on me because I was black and Bob was white and some judges were running scared.

I went to our bench and pulled on my sweatshirt. "Great race, Jack," someone called. I muttered an answer and sat with my head down between my knees. I waited for the relay call, not nervous, not anxious, not even interested anymore. I ran third, Bob was anchor. We were ahead when I passed him the baton, and he kept us there. So what?

I showered and dressed and shoved the medal into my pants pocket, wishing I had had the nerve to refuse it when it was first given to me. Now I had an idea that Bob wouldn't want it, either. I followed the rest of the team to the bus and climbed in. The bus groaned and coughed, backed up a bit and then swung out into heavy traffic. We were on our way home again.

The bus moved along smoothly and the yells and laughter finally settled into a steady buzz that increased in volume as we pulled up in front of the school. Cars were parked along the street in the darkness; friends and parents had come to meet us.

As I got in Pop's car, I saw Bob start off by himself. "Downey!" called the coach. I figured he would take Bob home and maybe talk about the meet and the medal and me on the way.

"Where's that medal?" asked Pop.

"In my pocket," I mumbled.

"In your pocket!" squealed Pop. "What's a first place medal doing in a pocket? Take it out and let me look at it."

I obeyed.

"I knew you'd beat that Downey fella," Pop said between happy chuckles. "What was your time? How far in front were you? Old Jack Rabbit Murray!" Pop punched me in the ribs as he talked. All the way home he was so busy laughing and talking that I didn't have to say anything. I just put my head back and waited for the sharp turn and rough bump that meant Pop had turned into our driveway.

Mom was waiting at the door. Ʌne looked at me as I walked up the steps.

"Didn't you win?" she asked.

"Sure," chuckled Pop. "He's got the medal right there in his hand."

I held it out and Mom took it for a moment.

"All that stew over a little piece of nothing," was what she said as she handed it back and went into the kitchen. We followed her.

"Want to eat, Jackie?" she asked. "I made cherry upside-down cake." I couldn't say no to that so she brought two big pieces, still warm and syrupy. She watched the way Pop killed his while I just poked at mine.

"What's the matter, son? Are you sick?" she asked.

"It's Bob," I answered.

Pop began to laugh. "What's the matter with him?" he sputtered. "Hasn't he crossed the finish line yet?" He fell back in his chair, knocked out over his own corny joke.

"Go on, Jackie," said Mom, frowning at Pop.

"*He* won it," I said. "Not me!"

"Then how come you got the medal?" Pop asked quickly.

"Well, the judges said I won, but I know Bob won. He hit the tape first." I couldn't even tell my own parents that I was given the medal just because I was black.

Pop was very positive now. "Listen," he said. "Down there in *that* place, if a judge said you won, he had good reason for saying it. You *won*, Jackie. You won."

I turned to Mom. "But it was Bob's best chance to get a scholarship," I told her.

Pop wouldn't be left out. "Any scholarship for running will go to you, Mr. Jack Rabbit. Downey will just have to look out for himself!"

"For goodness' sake, John, will you hush?" Mother said to him. He got a little bit mad and went out of the kitchen.

"Tell me about it, son," Mom said. She listened while I told her about Bob; how he ran without seeming to get any pleasure out of it; about the old man without legs who sewed Bob's clothes and about the cold air in the clean house. Pop came back and stood in the door, muttering and snorting, but I could tell that Mom understood.

"Go to bed," she told me. "Things may work out."

I was never more willing. I dropped the medal in my sock drawer and crawled into bed as quickly as possible. I could hear Mom and Pop talking while she washed the dishes. Her voice was soft and worried. His was loud.

"Jackie's really worried about that boy."

"Yep, but those are the breaks of life. 'Course, I'm beginning to feel kinda bad about the kid myself."

"I wish there was something we could do."

"*I* could. I guess I just could talk to Tom Linley about that boy."

"Tom Linley?"

"I told you about him before! Big wheel. The editor of the paper. He eats at my tables now."

Mom began washing pans and I couldn't hear her voice over the clatter.

But I heard Pop laugh proudly. "You'd be surprised at the pull we waiters have with the big boys. Sure ain't no point in *my* boy worrying himself sick about another kid when his old man can take over."

"What can you do?" Mom's voice was pretty high. She was used to Pop's schemes and sometimes she had to put a stop to them.

"I can do plenty. Ain't I Jack Murray, Senior? I'll make a bet with you that this Downey boy gets some kind of scholarship. No kidding!"

I have a lot of confidence in Pop even if he does get to me with his bragging. When he made that bet with Mom, I rolled over on my stomach and went to sleep.

For all his bragging, though, Pop never talked about his plans for Bob to me. But a couple of weeks before graduation, the Woodsfield Rotary Club made an announcement that, for the first time, it would grant a scholarship to some boy in our class who was an outstanding citizen, athlete, and scholar, with equal emphasis on all three.

And Bob Downey got it. Mr. Linley made the presentation on graduation night. When he shook Bob's hand Pop clapped so loud that people turned around to look at him.

Now Bob and I are both at State. I got the athletic scholarship that Pop wanted so badly. As for that medal they gave me at the State Finals? I'll never wear it. It isn't mine. But it means a lot to Pop and he thinks I won it fair. Maybe I'll give it to him!

The Diving Fool

by Franklin M. Reck

I STUMBLED on to "Sunny" Ray one afternoon in the pool at State College gym. I had just taken a dive — a front jacknife — and was hoisting myself over the edge of the tank when I caught a glimpse of a flashing white body bouncing off the end of the springboard and scooting up into the air. That was Sunny Ray, although I didn't know it then.

What caught my eye was the surprising height of his dive. I craned my neck around to see the finish of it. What I saw gave me a thrill. At the very top of his dive he bent easily at the hips and gracefully touched his

extended toes with his fingers. He opened out effort-
lessly and was perfectly straight before he entered the
water. The same dive I had just completed — only much
better done.

I climbed out of the pool and turned around to watch
for the unknown diver to appear. I was puzzled. I know
most of the divers in school. I'm the varsity diver myself. And no one I knew in school could do a front jackknife like the one I had just seen.

When the head finally bobbed up near the polished
nickel ladder, I saw a mouth framed for a laugh, and
a pair of alert, laughing eyes. A fun-loving face if ever
there was one. Not mischievous — but radiating fun.

I stepped on the board, feeling elated somehow, and
without a moment's hesitation performed a fairly difficult dive — a forward one-and-a-half. That's the one
where you make a complete somersault and a half and
enter the water headfirst. The moment I completed it,
I thrashed quickly to the ladder, climbed out dripping, and looked around at the board. "Fun-loving"
was just stepping forward, and in another instant he
was flying like a bird for the ceiling. High up, he
tucked, turned one and a half times and slanted for the
water like an arrow.

My, it was beautiful! There was a rollicking challenge in it too. Grinning, I strode out to the end of the
board and rose up on my toes with my back to the
water. Let "Fun-loving" try this one! Gathering all my
strength, I leaped backward and upward, at the same
time pulling up my knees to start my body on its whirl.

When the old sense of gravity gave me the order, I thrust out my hands backward and felt myself sliding into the water with a satisfying *suff!* A pretty good backward one-and-a-half, I thought, as I scudded for the edge of the pool. And a blasted difficult dive!

I glanced quickly at the board. Sure enough, there he was, poised with his back to the water and his arms extended for the jump — just as I had been a moment before. Up into the air he went. His smooth white body doubled into a knot, whirled too fast for the eye, and opened out into a perfect arch. In another instant his pointed toes had disappeared softly into the water.

The perfection of it choked me. Why wasn't he out for the varsity? I walked over to him, as he vaulted, catlike, out of the pool.

"My name's Weed," I said, sticking out my hand. "Art Weed."

He gave me a firm grip and grinned at me. "Mine's Donald Ray — for no good reason."

"I just wanted to say," I told him, "that I know about three more hard dives, but something tells me they wouldn't stump you. Who'd you dive for last?"

"Nobody."

I was surprised. "You mean to say you've never done any diving in competition?"

Ray shook his head.

"Where did you learn to dive?"

His face flushed at my abrupt question. "Oh, just — I don't know. At resorts and places."

"Freshman?"

"No. Second year. I came here from Simpson this fall."

"Why aren't you out for the varsity?"

"Why — I guess I never thought about it. Diving always seemed — well — fun. I've never taken it seriously."

"I think you ought to," I told him earnestly. "Why not be here tomorrow afternoon at three o'clock? That's when the varsity practices."

Ray's eyes lit up with pleasure. "Gosh — d'you think there's any use?"

I caught my chortle before it reached my lips. If he didn't know how good he was, I didn't intend to enlighten him. He'd find out soon enough.

"It won't hurt to try out, anyhow," I answered casually. "Will you be there?"

"Sure!" he came back eagerly.

"Don't forget." I smiled back at him as I started for the showers. He was looking at me, open-mouthed, face all alight. He didn't take his eyes off me until a group of fellows yelling "Sunny!" drew his attention.

"Sunny," I grinned. "Sunny Ray — Just fits him. Gosh, I like him."

I hurried through my dressing and hustled up to Coach Allen's office. Scotty Allen and I are good friends. I'd do a back jackknife off the Eiffel Tower into a bathtub, if he asked me to. He's a good hard driver, with a well-concealed sense of sympathy and an unfailing sense of humor.

I opened the door to his office and as I always do

when I'm keyed up, I tried to calm myself — stifle my feelings.

"Hello, Coach," I said very casually, as though I had just dropped in to pass the time of day.

"Hello yourself," answered Scotty, barely glancing up from the trial cards he was studying. "What are you so excited about? Has the United States declared war or something?"

"No," I replied. "Not since morning, anyway. I hate to disturb you, but I just dropped in to ask if you really wanted to win first at the Conference meet."

"I do have peculiar leanings that way," he smiled, still gazing at his trial cards. "But some of the other teams have the same silly idea — particularly Lawrence."

"Would first place in the dives help out any?"

"It would give us five points," he answered. "Why? Have you finally mastered that gainer one-and-a-half? I always said you had it in you — "

"Not me, Coach!" I blurted, joyously. "I know my limit. I know that Kramer of Lawrence, for one, can beat me easily. But I've just discovered a kid who can spot Kramer ten points and then wallop! Coach, he's — he's — "

Words failed me.

"He is, is he?" commented Scotty. "Where'd you stumble on to him?"

"In the pool, just a half hour ago. Saw him do a front jack, a forward one-and-a-half, and — gosh — Coach, his front jack would take him over a bar twelve feet above the pool. No kidding! And — "

"Does he keep his feet together?"

"Yes, sir! And his toes pointed. And he arches with his stomach instead of his chest — "

The coach began to look interested. I ran on.

"He's taller than I am, and graceful as a cat! He's a diving fool!"

I was just beaming, I guess, because Scotty smiled at me appreciatively. "When do I get a look at this marvel?"

"At practice tomorrow. He's eligible for the varsity, too, because he's had a year at Simpson! Wait until you see him!"

"I hope he's as good as you say he is," said Scotty, looking at me quizzically. Then he leaned my way confidentially. "I've just come from a meeting of the Athletic Council. We went over the plans for the new field house, and the Council wants to build the pool with only five hundred seats."

"Holy smokes!" I couldn't believe it. "Is that all?"

"There ought to be two thousand seats!" exploded Scotty. His lips closed in a thin line. "I'd give my right eye to win that Conference — show 'em! And a first in the dives would be a godsend. The Athletic Council ought to wake up!"

"Sunny Ray's your man," I said gleefully. "Unless I'm blind as well as cockeyed, there's no diver in this Conference can beat him."

"How about second place too?" Scotty asked, looking at me intently.

I blushed. I'm only an ordinary diver, and the coach

knows it. I just haven't the brilliance — the flash — that
Kramer of Lawrence has, or Sunny Ray.

"I'll knock off my usual fourth place."

"Somebody ought to knock off your block!" he
snorted.

I laughed. Scotty was always prodding me to be better than I was, and I was always trying. But it was like
trying to make a silk ear out of a sow's purse — or
whatever it is. I could be fairly good, but never sensa-
tional.

The next afternoon, at three, I undressed in record
time and fairly flew down the steps leading to the
p ' Frank Richardson and Jack Crandall, our two
dash men, were already in the water, thrashing out
their twenty laps. Several others of the squad were chat-
ting and laughing near the springboard. The coach
wasn't down yet.

Over in the corner, sitting on a canvas chair and
studying his curled-up toes, was Sunny Ray. I walked
over to him.

"'Smatter, Ray," I grinned, "is your lunch doing
handsprings?"

"No, I just — " His face was a little pale. "I never did
anything like this before."

"Don't worry," I reassured him. "It's just practice."

I knew what Sunny's feelings were. Fancy-diving is
the tensest, most nerve-racking, kind of competitive
sport. When you want to vent your energy strenuously,
you've got to pose delicately — to make every move
just so. And hovering over you, every minute, is the spec-

ter of a flop. Sunny, for the first time, was beginning to realize all this. I looked down and saw that he was shivering almost imperceptibly.

"Better take a practice dive," I suggested. "Start the old circulation."

"I — I guess I'll wait a while," he replied.

Just then, Scotty came into the pool. I trotted over to him, brought him to the corner, and introduced Sunny.

"Just a minute," the coach smiled, "until I put this gang to work."

A few minutes later, after he had started the distance men on their long grind, Scotty turned to us.

"All right, Art," he called, "go through your dives. You follow him, Ray."

I slapped Sunny on the back. "Give it all you've got," I whispered, and then started for the board.

I completed my swan dive — it felt like a good one — and clambered out of the water to watch Sunny. He was standing halfway up the board, nervously rubbing his hands together. He dropped his hands to his side, clenched them involuntarily, and started. Three steps up the board, a short final leap, and Sunny was traveling skyward. His head was back, his arms outspread, and his body perfectly arched. But just at the top of his dive, he broke — bent at the hips — and dropped headfirst into the pool.

"Gosh, Coach," I murmured, "that'll happen to anybody. He tried to go too high and had to bend to get down."

Scotty nodded. I went nervously to the board for my

second dive while Sunny was climbing out of the pool. I was terrifically anxious for him to make good — to dive as beautifully as he had yesterday.

But he didn't. I don't mean that he flopped completely. He just didn't go quite so high, didn't turn so swiftly, didn't enter the water so cleanly. He was intent, serious, and just a bit uncertain. His last dive was the back one-and-a-half, and he splashed quite a bit of water on it. I turned to the coach. He looked entirely unconvinced.

"You wait," I said earnestly. "You haven't seen anything."

"He'll make a pretty fair diver," Scotty said gently. "He's a bit green."

I felt like shouting: "Fair diver! He's a natural-born champion!" But I knew there had been no evidence of it today.

In the next two practices — the last two before the dual meet at Lawrence — Sunny improved only slightly. He was trying desperately hard, but the realization that he was diving before critical eyes seemed to upset him. He couldn't call out the bounding, carefree brilliance that was somewhere inside of him. On Friday the team left for Lawrence, and Sunny Ray stayed behind.

We lost the Lawrence meet by a heartbreaking score — 35-33. I placed second in the dives to Kramer. Kramer is a marvelously flashing performer — just like Sunny was the first time I saw him.

"I wish I could dive like Kramer!" I confided to the coach on the train going home, "Isn't he beautiful? But — he's no better than Sunny. Not so good."

I said it challengingly, but I didn't get a rise out of Scotty. He just looked at me oddly.

During the next week Scotty began driving the squad. The Conference meet was only three weeks away, and there was one more hard duel — with Tech. So far we had lost only the one meet, and we had a fair chance for the big title. We worked like blazes and were happy. I had double duty — practicing dives and working out for the relay.

On the Thursday before the Tech meet I got down to practice early. Sunny was already in the pool.

" 'Lo, early bird!" I yelped. "Found any worms?"

"Fat, woolly ones," retorted Ray. "They're all gone. You might as well trot back to your nest."

"You don't trot to a nest," I reproved him. "You fly. And here goes!"

I stepped on the board and did my swan dive.

"That wasn't high enough," chided Sunny. "You should fly like an *iggle*. This way."

High up into the air he soared, like a zooming sea gull. I whistled. *That* was something like!

"When an iggle has corns on his feet," grinned Sunny, vaulting out of the water, "he flies above a mounting and scratches 'em — like this."

Three slow steps, that predatory pounce on the end of the board, and he was again shooting for the ceiling. Away up there, he quickly jacked, touched his toes with his hands, and dropped. Straight as a plumb line. No splash.

I chuckled joyfully.

"What happens," I asked him with mock seriousness, "when an iggle has a cramp?"

"He makes for a cloud," Sunny replied lightly, "and doubles up. Poor iggle."

Again he sailed skyward. Unbelievably high up he tucked, turned one and a half times and zipped for the water. I was seeing the real Sunny now!

"Don't mind me," I told him weakly. "I'm just a ground hog."

He made a couple of mysterious passes at me with his hands.

"Now," he announced in a deep, formal tone, "you're a naviator. A naviator hunting iggles. Chase me."

For a quarter of an hour we played our game. Sunny's face was all alight. He wasn't on inspection now — he was disporting himself naturally and joyously.

"What do you two think you are," grunted Frank Richardson, who had just come in, "a couple of bounding porpoises?"

"Porpoises!" I bellowed. "He called us porpoises! Tell him what we are, Sunny!"

"We're iggles," grinned Sunny.

"We live in igloos," I added.

"And spend all our time iggling."

Frank Richardson backed away from us slightly in awe.

I turned to Sunny. "He doesn't understand," I murmured. "He's an eel."

"And eels," finished Sunny, "can't speak igglish."

Chortling, he ran to the board and did another perfect one-and-a-half.

I sensed that somebody was standing close to me, and I turned around to see Scotty looking intently at the ripples that marked the end of Sunny's uncannily beautiful dive.

"I've been watching from the balcony," the coach said in my ear. "I'm beginning to understand."

"Wasn't that wonderful?" I gulped. "He's a diving fool, isn't he?"

Scotty didn't answer, but his eyes were shining.

I didn't sleep much that night. For about a half hour I lay in bed thinking about Sunny's performance. Then it occurred to me that he was the man to go to Tech with the team tomorrow night. I wasn't particularly needed on the relay. Either Wilson or Harwood could take my place. And the coach couldn't take more than ten men.

The next morning, between clas.es, I went up to Scotty's office. I knew he'd be in because he has swimming classes in the morning. He was studying those time cards of his.

"If you're trying to figure out why you should take two divers to Tech, you can quit," I told him. "I've got two exams next Monday, and I'd be just as well satisfied if you'd let me stay home."

The coach looked at me thoughtfully. "Do you think you could win first at Tech?"

I had a good laugh. The same story.

"I *know* Sunny can win first. That boy — " Thinking of those dives he made yesterday left me speechless.

Scotty looked straight at the wall in front of him. I began to get fidgety — to feel that I had spoken out of turn. "I don't mean," I explained hastily, "that I don't want to go! I do — but — "

"Might as well break Sunny in," Scotty interrupted. "You'd better take a workout while we're gone."

I had a sudden glimpse of that rollicking squad of mermen cutting up on the train and me sitting around the fraternity house.

"I will," I replied, getting to my feet and walking unsteadily to the door. "I — I'll take a workout tomorrow afternoon."

That night, when I saw the gang off at the train, Sunny drew me aside.

"Gee whiz, Art," he blurted out, "this isn't right."

I grinned. "The best man wins, Sunny." I roughed him up a bit, to steer him away from anything sentimental.

"B-but," he said, holding me off, "I'm not sure I'm the best man."

"You've never seen yourself dive!" I chuckled.

That night, at the fraternity house, several of the brothers wanted to know why I wasn't out of town with the team.

"Trying out a new diver," I explained. "Sunny Ray." "Is he good?"

"He's the coming Conference champion," I asserted with conviction.

"Heck," mourned one of the fellows. "I thought we had the coming champ right here in the house!"

"Don't be funny," I grunted.

Saturday morning I had a couple of classes. In the

afternoon I went down to the pool and punished the springboard savagely. In the evening I went to the movies and saw nothing on the screen except my mind's picture of the State College team battling Tech — of Sunny soaring upward. After the show I hurried to the *Campus Daily* office to get the results.

"We won, 40 to 28," Spike Hanlon, the sporting editor informed me, as he handed me the summary.

I scanned it eagerly to see how Sunny had come out in the dives. Halfway down was this paragraph:

Fancy Dives: First, Marlowe, Tech, 108.6; second, Floyd, Tech, 102; third, Ray, State College, 96.

Sunny had flopped! I knew what had happened as though I'd been there. I could almost feel the coldness that possessed Sunny's knees the first time he walked out to the board before a thousand rooters and three judges.

"Just the same," I murmured, "he's the greatest natural diver I've ever seen. And he's going to win first at the Conference!"

Monday afternoon, as I went into the locker room to undress, the coach called me. He led me up to his office, where he drew up a second chair and motioned me to sit down.

For a couple of minutes he scribbled busily on a sheet of paper, and then he shoved it over to me.

"Barring upsets," he said, briefly, "that's how things will stack up at the Conference meet."

This is what he'd written on the sheet:

	Lawrence	State Col.	Others
200 yd. relay	5	3	3
50 yd. dash	3	5	3
100 yd. dash	3	5	3
150 yd. backstroke	3	2	6
200 yd. breaststroke	3	2	6
440 yd. swim	2	8	1
300 yd. medley relay	5	1	5
	—	—	—
	24	26	27
Dives	—	—	—

"We'll take first in the 50 and the 100, and we'll sweep the four-forty," he said. "Lawrence will take the relay and push us in the dashes. We haven't got a chance in the medley — we may take a fourth. Which means that the dives will tell the story. You and Sunny —" he paused.

I knew how much the coach wanted to win the Conference. The Athletic Council was disposed to regard swimming lightly. And now, with the plans for the new field house under consideration, swimming at State College was at the crossroads. I had two visions — one of a spacious pool, built to accommodate thousands of rooters; another of an ordinary pool, around which a narrow bank of spectators sat hemmed in by walls.

"I haven't said much to the Athletic Council," Scotty said, reading my thoughts, "because I wouldn't have been listened to. But if we win the Conference, I will talk — and I'll get a respectful hearing."

I cleared my throat huskily. "It's up to Sunny and me, isn't it?"

"All out for the fancy dives!" bawled the announcer. Sunny's face paled.

"Come on, Sunny," I said calmly. "You need a bath — it's Saturday night."

The squad milled around us, helping us off with the bathrobes and slapping us on the back. I hoped fervently that Sunny wasn't taking to heart their tense, eager expressions. Every face said: "It's up to you!"

Diving is a terrific test of a man's nerves. When your muscles are crying out for vigorous action, you've got to restrain them. Thousands of eyes are glued on you. You're the star performer, in a spotlight. And the slightest misstep, the least error in timing, may cause your downfall!

Sunny's voice called me out of my nerve-racking thoughts.

"Are we going to t-take a practice dive?" he asked.

I squared my shoulders. I had a job to do. *This meet was up to me!*

"No," I replied seriously. "I'm an iggle."

"Wh-what?"

"I'm an iggle," I repeated, "and an iggle never dives. He swoops. Swatch me."

Without looking back at Sunny, I walked up to the board and took my first practice dive — a swan. As I climbed out of the water, I noticed the coach looking at me with a confident smile. I walked back to where Sunny was standing rubbing his thighs.

"I tried to swash that beam up there with my tail feathers," I told him, "but I missed it. Heck."

Sunny grinned at me for the first time that night.

"No wonder," he said, starting for the board. "Your tail feathers have moulted."

My heart bounded. Sunny at least had a comeback! I watched him eagerly as he poised and started forward. He sailed up — not quite as high as I could have wished, but still better than I had expected.

I racked my brains for my next line. As he came up to me, dripping, I smiled.

"You swished it," I said, "with a swooping swish. I'm going after it with a swipping swoop."

A little weak that remark, I thought dolefully, as I strode up and took my second practice — a running half gainer. Streaming wet, I clambered out and walked back to Sunny, putting on an expression of mock disgust.

"I swipped too hard," I grunted, "and got all dusty."

"I swish I could swoop like that," he said grinning.

I chuckled joyously. Kramer, the Lawrence diver, walking past us to the board, looked at us in dumb amazement. After Kramer, Sunny started up.

"If you get dusty, swoop down and swash," I cautioned.

"All right," he chuckled. "Here goes for a swishing swoop."

"A swipping, soaring swoosh!" I encouraged him.

I could have wept with pure joy. His one-and-a-half was a thing of beauty, and I knew then that everything was all right. There'd be just one more crisis — when the clerk called Sunny for his first official dive. Our nonsense chatter — silly as it seemed — was working on Sunny's naturally buoyant spirit.

"You fellows had enough practice?" an official near us inquired.

We nodded. I felt a tightening in my throat.

A man with a megaphone walked to the edge of the pool.

"The next event," he sang out to the crowd, "is the fancy dive. Each man is required to do four dives — the plain front, the plain back, the front jackknife and the back jackknife. After that, he does four difficult dives of his own choosing! First man up, Kramer of Lawrence. The plain front!"

Kramer did a good dive — too good for our comfort — and won a storm of applause.

"Ray! State College!" bellowed the announcer.

This, for me, was the critical point. Sunny's first dive!

"That beam, iggle," I whispered to him solicitously, "is still dusty."

"Sawful," he whispered back, "I'll swish it."

Sunny went so high on that dive that I was afraid he'd have to break. But he didn't. At the very top of his dive, his feet rose gracefully toward the ceiling, his back perfectly arched every moment. And again, that smooth entry into the water!

He walked back to me with a light-hearted grin, the water streaming from his hair.

"Did I get it?" he asked.

"Every speck," I gurgled. "I'll go up and polish it." I felt supremely confident now. Sunny, I felt sure, was going to come through!

And I was right. Every time he stepped on the board,

he grew better. Not an uncertain step. No sudden hes-
itancy. And, all through it, we played our game. The
crowd, the sober-faced judges with their pads, the loud
applause meant nothing to us. We were too intent upon
sweeping that skyward beam immaculately clean.
Weren't we iggles? Iggles cannot be bothered with
mundane things. They dust the mountaintops!

I looked over to where our squad was sitting, noticed the look of awe on Frank Richardson's face and
the happy smile on Scotty's lean countenance.

Sunny's last dive — that marvelously sinuous thing
of flashing turns called the gainer one-and-a-half —
brought a spontaneous outburst from the crowd. Not
another diver had done so well — I felt sure of it.

Dripping and content, our play of iggles ended, we
walked back to the bench. The coach bounded forward
to meet us.

"Fine work, Sunny," he said warmly. Then he turned
to me.

"Art," he grinned, "I didn't think you had it in you."

"It worked," I bubbled happily. "Didn't it?"

The coach just looked at me, his face alight. The
rest of the squad pulled us to the bench, wrapping our
bathrobes about us, and rubbed our legs and arms with
towels, meanwhile babbling joyfully in our ears.

I didn't respond to their outburst because I was trying to figure the status of the meet. The results of the
dives would not be announced until after the medley
race was finished — that was the last event. Sunny's
first and my fourth — if I was that lucky — would give

us six points. Kramer of Lawrence had most certainly won second. That would make the score 29 to 24 in our favor. Lawrence would win first in the medley. 29 to 29! We had to have a fourth in the medley!

But we didn't get it. We were shut out completely, I felt sick at heart. That glorious diving — for nothing. . . .

"While we're waiting for the results of the fancy dives," called an announcer, "I'll read you the status of the meet so far. Lawrence, 26, State College, 23 — " As the announcer read off the other scores, a clerk walked up to him with a sheet of paper. I gripped Sunny's arm hard.

"Results of the fancy dives!" bawled the megaphone. "Ah-ha! You'd never guess!"

"First — " came from the megaphone " — Weed, State College, 108.4."

I almost fell off the bench. Me — me? A wave of handclapping pelted the walls.

— "Second, Donald Ray, State College, 103.2 — "

Another wave of handclapping. Unaware of what I was doing, I got to my feet.

"He's — he's cockeyed!" I yelled. Unfortunately, I had picked a dead calm in which to give utterance to my thoughts. The crowd tittered.

"I'm cockeyed!" the announcer sing-songed. "I'll have to have my eyes examined. Third, Kramer, Lawrence, 99.8. Fourth, Marlowe, Tech, 94. Fifth, Hendricks, Cole, 91.5. Final results of the meet: State College, 31, Lawrence, 28 — "

I didn't hear the rest of it, because about eight husky swimmers were trying to pull me apart. Still dazed, I jerked myself free and walked to the coach. It wasn't right — I'm just not good enough to beat Sunny and Kramer!

"Sunny won those dives, Coach," I protested. But he just grinned at me. I felt the need of explaining myself.

"It worked out just as we planned," I elaborated painfully. "I did what you said — talked him into it — "

"*You talked yourself into it,* you diving fool," laughed Scotty. "Haven't I been telling you all season you had it in you?"

I just stared at him, and if I looked as dumb as I felt, I must have been a sight. *Me.* Conference Champion.

"Nope," I said, positively. "There's something wrong."

Sunny had his arm around my shoulder, and now he tightened it, chuckling.

"You've never seen yourself dive, iggle," he said.